The Gandhian Adventures of Raj & Iqbal

About the Book

Meet Raj Kumar Reddy and his best friend and brother in life, Iqbal Ali Mohammad Khan . . .

They are Gandhians—followers of Mahatma Gandhi, lovers of peace, and seekers of the truth. They live in that greatest city of Mumbai, and their lives are simple and calm. But things change when they decide to seek the truth about onion prices in India.

As their journey gets increasingly surreal, they meet an Indian freedom fighter presumed dead in 1945, learn the secret to wrinkle-free skin, and finally embark on a dangerously silly encounter with a Pakistani extremist group on the high seas off the coast of India.

About the Author

Zubin J. Shroff writes eclectic, entertaining, 200-page novels, many of which contain elements of satire, drama, and surrealism.

He was born in 1975 in India, and he studied the sciences at the Cathedral School in Mumbai, philosophy at Lawrence University in Wisconsin, and the fine arts (of business) at Columbia University in New York City. He lives in Minnesota, USA.

Learn more about Zubin, his books, and his very nice mailing list at zubinjshroff.com.

Novels by Zubin J. Shroff

Weather Report

The Gandhian Adventures of Raj & Iqbal

The Last Free Man

The Land of 9,999 Lakes

The Hoppers Romanov (An American Love Story)

Genesis

Sick

Cry

The Marriage of Percy and Pigeon

Cowgirl

Bad Dog

zubinjshroff.com/novels

The Gandhian Adventures of Raj & Iqbal

a novel

Zubin J. Shroff

Four Circle Press
Minneapolis

The Gandhian Adventures of Raj & Iqbal: A Novel

Cover Art by August West
Book Design by Jack & Betty Frost

Set in Caslon

Published by Four Circle Press
Minneapolis, MN 55458-0442
First Edition, 2011

ISBN: 978-1-937308-17-9 (alk. paper)
ISBN: 978-1-937308-01-8 (ebook)

10 9 8 7 6 5 4 3 2 1

www.zubinjshroff.com
www.fourcirclepress.com

The Gandhian Adventures of Raj & Iqbal

I

Hello hello good morning. RK here. How are you all? Me, I am fine. I am sitting here writing to you all so that everyone can understand what has happened with us. Oh, sorry. Now Iqbal is poking me and saying I am taking up all the attention. But I warned him this would happen when we made the agreement. The agreement that whoever does the typing work, he gets to put his name first. Okay fine, he is poking me again so I will introduce him. I will introduce my brother.

Iqbal is my brother in life. Iqbal Ali Mohammad Khan. But call him Iqbal. And call me RK, short for Raj Kumar. Raj Kumar Reddy.

We are both Gandhians. Peace-lovers. Lovers of peace. We are true Gandhians. At least true in spirit and intention if not yet in body and action. You see, I only say that because when we ultimately finished reading the full autobiography of Bapu, we realized that to be true Gandhians we must also be the Brahmacharis. Means what? Means that we must let go of the sexual desire. Let that energy be diverted into the eternal quest for the truth.

So we told this to our wives. First they laughed at us. But now . . . actually now they still laugh at us. Because after we made this pledge we experienced increase in urges to do the opposite. It is the funny reaction like how if a child has not played with a toy for a long time and you try and take the toy away then immediately the child wants to play only with that toy. Now every day the wives laugh and say they are getting more bedroom action than ever before. It seems this pledge of celibacy has backfired in a not displeasurable way. But never mind. It is part of the challenge, we believe. After all, Bapu himself did not overcome the challenge until almost forty years of age. And we are not yet forty. Still one or two or three more years until that age. So we have time to meet this challenge.

But anyway. That challenge is not the reason we are writing this. Naturally we will update you on our progress to Brahmachari in case others find inspiration. But the true reason for writing down our stories is not such a personal business. It is a public matter. It is a matter of utmost seriousness and importance. It is a matter of the highest truth.

Let us explain how this thing started.

All big things start as small things. Okay okay, maybe not all things. Some things may start big only. But anyway, this is not one of those things that started big. It started small, and then got bigger. Make no mistake, we made no mistake. Our intention only was to start small and then get big. But what seemed small at first was bigger than we thought. Then, as we proceeded, what we thought was big suddenly became massive. Massive, I tell you.

And that is why we must put down everything on paper. And using English, even though Hindi or Urdu would be more poetic to our own minds. Iqbal is nodding. We could write this in Hindi or Urdu, does not matter which. Both are sister languages. Sisters, like we are brothers. But we must write with English because these matters are bigger than us. They are bigger than Mumbai. They are bigger than Maharashtra. They are bigger than India. They are massive. Massive, I tell you.

But of course we must start with the small thing. The small thing that began us on our Gandhian adventures.

Any Gandhian adventure can only have a single item as the goal. Truth is that item. Truth is that goal. The whole point of being a Gandhian is to pursue the truth wherever she may lie. Or he. Whatever gender the truth is. And wherever he or she may be hiding. Actually it is better we think of truth as genderless. So to rephrase in genderless language: As Gandhians we are automatically dedicated to the pursuit of truth wherever it may be hiding or whatever it is.

This seemed like a simple and honorable goal, and so me and Iqbal were happy. But then one day Iqbal joined me for tea and he put on a very worried face. I asked him what is wrong, and he said that how can we say we are pursuing truth if we do nothing but drink tea and go to office for eight hours and drink tea and eat dinner and love our families? And since last year our children are also away from home and now living in college hostels. And so, Iqbal said with his worried face, how can we say we are in pursuit of truth?

So I said the problem is the word pursuit. If we say pursuit, then we must pursue. And if we are not pursuing, then we cannot say we are in pursuit.

And then Iqbal smiled and said yes, that is the problem.

So I said should we change the word? Should we replace the word pursuit with a less active word? Perhaps we say our goal is the acceptance, not pursuit, of truth. That way we can drink tea and go to office and drink tea and eat food and love our wives. And when the truth comes, we will simply accept it.

Iqbal stopped smiling and said no. I did not ask him why because I knew why. Iqbal and me are brothers in life after all. Our thought patterns are one and the same.

So before the tea had even cooled we had made the decision. To pursue the truth wherever it is hiding means only one thing. It means we must go out and look for it. Look for the truth. If the truth is hiding, then it must be found. And as Gandhians it is our sworn duty to find the truth. Indeed, as Gandhians it is our only duty.

And so this small realization, this small thing that came to us even before the tea had cooled, this was the beginning. The beginning of our Gandhian adventures.

2

Our first day of pursuing the truth started off quite inauspiciously. It rained even though monsoons were over. Of course, we are Mumbaikars, and therefore we love the rain, but today it was not so much enjoyment. You see, it rained enough to cause little flooding and confusion and bus delays, but it did not rain enough to cause offices to be declared bandh. I mean closed. But no matter. I telephoned the office and said I have bus trouble, and so I'll not be coming to office today. Then I telephoned my brother Iqbal and said to him he should do the same and then come over to my place for some tea and we will watch the rain from my balcony.

Iqbal sounded very much in hurry mode, and he said he already called office and said there is bus trouble. So I said why is there reason to hurry then? He said there is no hurry.

But I know when Iqbal is in hurry mode. He speaks very very fast and his breath becomes very very loud. And today on the telephone I could easily tell he was in hurry mode. So I said to Iqbal that he is my brother in life and I can easily tell he is in hurry mode, so he might as well tell me the problem. Maybe even I can help.

Then Iqbal says no-no, no help needed. It's a small problem.

So I said what problem?

And he said not to worry, it is a small problem.

So again I asked Iqbal, what is the problem?

And then he tells me that yesterday night his lovely wife asked him to bring onions, and he said no problem, he will do it after watching the TV serial, but then after the serial he felt tired and said to himself quietly that he will wake up early and get onions. And then after going to the bedroom his wife asks him if he brought onions, and Iqbal said yes because he thought he would bring the onions early in the morning, and so no problem. It is as if the onions are already there. But then in the morning not only did Iqbal wake up late, but the rains were coming down and he could not see the vegetablewalla across the street.

So now there were no onions, and Iqbal was in hurry mode.

And this is what I meant when I said earlier that our first day of pursuing the truth started inauspiciously. Our first day of Gandhian pursuit of truth started with three lies total between me and Iqbal. Three lies, and one small problem.

The onion problem.

When I reflected on Iqbal's onion problem, I immediately became anxious. After all, an onion problem is never a small problem in India. Governments have fallen because of onion problem. Murders have been committed because of onion problem. Suicides have occurred because of onion problem. Families are every day being destroyed due to onion problem. And these are just the facts. The rumors are much, much worse.

They say that the 1947 partition between India and Pakistan was thirty-five percent due to onion problem. The current border disputes with China are minimum eighty percent related to onion problem. After all, China is the number one producer of onion and India is number two. Same with population rankings. We are both competitive nations, and so every comparison must be taken seriously. Onion requires land area for cultivation, and therefore any land dispute is almost definitely related to desire to move ahead in the onion rankings.

So I quickly finished my tea and toast and biscuit and took bath and then informed my wife that I was leaving to help Iqbal move ahead of China in the onion ranking. My wife looked at me and said okay go but telephone me if you'll not be here for lunch.

So I set off in my rain-sandals and with my black umbrella and went to Iqbal's building, which is down the lane from me. Very close. Close like we are brothers. Iqbal lives on the third floor and so I took the lift up to the third floor and was surprised to see my brother sitting on the stairs leading to the fourth floor. He looked very sad and told me his wife had pushed him out of the house. I did not ask why, because I knew why.

Onion problem.

So I said no problem. I am here, no? Solution is simple. We are to go find some onions. What is there to feel sad about?

Then Iqbal said that he had gone down to the vegetablewalla and gone behind the shop to see if he was there. It turned out the vegetablewalla was there, but he was going to open late today because he did not have much goods. The vegetable delivery had not come today. So Iqbal had explained his situation and requested to purchase onions before the shop opened. The vegetablewalla shook his head and nodded and smiled and apologized. Then he said onions are restricted today, and therefore the price will be 140 rupees per kilogram.

I was hit by price shock and immediately sat down near Iqbal. Impossible, I said. Our vegetablewalla would not say such a thing. Why, I asked Iqbal, you have had some argument with him or what? He is spiting you in this emergency situation?

Iqbal said no, no problem. In fact, the vegetablewalla was sad to do so but said he had no choice.

No choice means what? I asked Iqbal.

Iqbal said he did not ask because he was so upset. He came back up and sat on the stairs to the fourth floor. And then I came.

So I said we will find out. Let us go talk to the vegetablewalla and find out what is the onion problem.

3

The vegetablewalla was very sad and worried just like us, but he cannot do anything about onion problem, he said. It is out of his hands, he said. Wholesale onion prices have increased to almost 120 rupees per kilogram, so how can he sell for less than 140 rupees? Little profit at least must be there, no? Onions are main source of profit because onions are bought every day by every family without fail. Except for some Jain families, of course. They do not eat onions and so they do not buy. But that is not the point. The point is that onion wholesale price has increased by hundreds of percents.

So we asked the vegetablewalla how this could be.

He answered that it is a simple case of supply and demand.

Iqbal and I looked at each other and we nodded in acceptance and we stood up to go away. Then we looked at each other again and remembered that we have made the decision that we will not simply accept the truth. No. Acceptance is not good enough. Pursuit must be made.

So we sat down again near the vegetablewalla, one on each side of him. We loudly proclaimed that we will not rest until the truth is found. And so we demanded the truth. What is meant by simple case of supply and demand?

Vegetablewalla said sorry, I am only a simple vegetablewalla. I do not understand such complicated matters. Why are you putting such complex questions to such a simple man? You both are office goers. You must have gone to school. And yet you ask these tough questions of me? Get out, you bloody bastards. Leave me alone. Onion price is now 145 rupees for you. Special price for bastards. Now get out. Bastards.

So immediately Iqbal and I got out. Typically we would have not stood to be called such names. One tight slap he would have received. One from Iqbal and one from me. Two slaps total. But not today. Gandhians do not deliver slaps to others. Especially active Gandhians such as Iqbal and myself. So we immediately removed ourselves from the situation.

Now what to do? The rain had stopped and traffic problems seemed to be better. But onion problem was still big. Bigger even. Now what?

Iqbal was standing and thinking very hard. I know Iqbal's thinking stance. He puts one leg on something, like a stool or chair or bench, in this case bench because no stool or chair was available. Then he puts one elbow on the knee of the leg that is on the stool or chair or bench. In this case bench.

So I inquired about the status of his thought. Iqbal touched his beard and moved his head. He said that he remembers his schooling but does not remember about supply and demand. So now what to do?

I said I do not know. I do not even remember my schooling.

Then Iqbal smiled and exited from his thoughtful stance. He said yes. I have it.

I said what is it you have?

Iqbal said idea. I have idea. We will ask the schoolmaster.

What schoolmaster? I said. But then I remembered. Iqbal's son's old schoolmaster lives not far. He is retired and gives only tuitions to five or six boys and maybe girls. So I said wonderful. Let us go to the schoolmaster.

And Iqbal touched his beard and led the way. I smiled and followed with my black umbrella. Now the pursuit had really begun.

4

The schoolmaster was giving tuitions when we arrived. We waited in the hall and his wife sent tea for us. We drank tea and waited.

The schoolmaster finally came out to the hall and saw us. He called for more tea. We waited while the schoolmaster drank the tea. Then he asked us what the problem is.

We said onion problem.

Immediately his face turned into a worried face. He quickly stood up and rushed out of the hall. I looked at Iqbal but Iqbal did not look at me. Iqbal stared at the doorway from the hall to the kitchen. I leaned over to see, and what I saw made me scared.

Schoolmaster was in the kitchen with a big knife. He was waving the knife at the cook. Schoolmaster looked very angry.

Not normal angry, but serious angry. I said to Iqbal, should we go? He said yes, definitely. So we got up to go.

Before that could happen the schoolmaster returned to the hall. He did not have the knife and so we stood quietly. He looked okay so we sat down again.

Sorry, said the schoolmaster, but when you said onion problem I remembered that today I am having a small get-together for my tuition children. These youngsters like the pizza, so I had instructed the cook to make pizza snack. High onion content, of course. But when you said onion problem I had to go and stop the cook from cutting the onions. Because now if there is onion problem, then value per onion immediately increases. It is a simple case of supply and demand.

Immediately Iqbal and I perked up. Supply and demand, we said, that is why we have come. Then we asked the schoolmaster to explain. So he explained.

Now see, he said, supply of onions changes from month to month and year to year. Sometimes it increases. Sometimes it decreases. But demand for onions does not change so much. And even when demand changes, it changes in only one way. By increasing.

So we said how is that? Is it because the Jains are losing their faith and increasing their onion demands? Is this the problem? The Jains are causing onion problems with their demands?

No no, said the schoolmaster. Jains are not creating any onion demand. Increase in onion demand comes from increase in population of Mumbai.

So why not simply decrease the population of Mumbai, I

said. Iqbal shook his head, but it was too late. I had already said it.

Stupid man you are, said the schoolmaster. He became irritated. There is some button for population decrease, or what? Stupid bugger.

I felt very bad. I said sorry.

Then Iqbal spoke up. Why not increase the supply of onion, he said.

Schoolmaster nodded. Yes, that is smarter. But it is not easy. Supply of onion can only be increased in one of two ways. One way is to increase yield of onion.

Means what? I said.

Means you must try and enhance the onion so that more onions can be grown per hectare per year.

Enhance? Impossible, I said. Onion is perfect, therefore it cannot be enhanced, and so increasing the onion's yield must be a futile task. The onion's state of perfection can be inferred by its round bulbous form, since roundness is a sign of perfection. I rubbed my round head and smiled. Now the schoolmaster cannot call me a stupid bugger.

But the schoolmaster slapped my round stomach quite hard and told me to be quiet. Stupid bastard, he said. You shut up.

I almost got angry, but Iqbal gave me a look and I remembered our goal. We are in the pursuit of truth, and in that pursuit we may have to bear hardships and suffering, and so I will bear up.

The schoolmaster continued. Your reasoning is incorrect, but your conclusion is approximately correct. Onion yields cannot be increased much more. They have increased over the years, but now we are achieving diminishing returns to scale.

Means what, said Iqbal.

Means that onion yields can now only be increased very slightly and only with great effort. Whereas previously onion yields could be increased greatly with only slight effort.

Iqbal nodded that he understood.

I nodded also, even though I did not understand. But if one of us understands, then it is okay, I think. Plus, after all that tea and biscuits, I could not take much more abuse to the stomach.

Iqbal said fine, then what is the other option for increasing onion supply?

Other way is to increase the amount of hectares used for onion cultivation, said the schoolmaster.

Now I knew the answer for sure. I spoke up. So we must reclaim land from Pakistan and Bangladesh and China, I said.

The schoolmaster looked at me. That is one way, he said. But it is a stupid way. Most of the land bordering Pakistan and China is very cold and mountainous. Not good for onion.

Then Bangladesh, I said.

Maybe Bangladesh, said the schoolmaster. But there will be flooding problems. Okay for rice. Not so okay for onion. No, there are two other ways to increase onion growing area without annexation of neighboring countries.

What other ways, said Iqbal.

The schoolmaster lifted his finger. One way is to simply expand onion cultivation into places where currently nothing is being cultivated. But this is tough. Not much suitable land is available now, he said.

Then what? I said.

Last way is to reduce the land used by other things and divert it to onion usage.

You mean like reduce tomato crop and increase onion crop by replacing tomato fields with onion fields? Like that? I said.

Yes, said the schoolmaster.

But this requires comparison of onion with other vegetables. How to decide, said Iqbal.

It is not easy, said the schoolmaster. It requires judgment.

I shook my head. No judgment required, I said. If onion is perfect, then there is no comparison with other vegetables. We can pick up any vegetable and replace with onion.

The schoolmaster looked at me. You are a stupid bugger, he said. Nothing is perfect. Not even onion.

Now I was quite unhappy, and maybe even a little angry. So I looked at the schoolmaster with my unhappy and slightly angry face. So what now, I said. How can we compare two imperfect things with one another? Speak up now, O Mister Smart One. So what is the answer?

The schoolmaster raised his hand to slap me but I was too quick and I jumped to my feet. Unfortunately, in doing so I knocked the tray from the table and the nice tea set fell to the clean tiles on the floor. Of course, the tea set broke into pieces. Every element of the tea set broke—cups, saucers, tea pot, even the spoons.

Iqbal, my brother in life, snatched me by the hand and pulled me out of harm's way. And in this case the harm was coming directly from the schoolmaster, and directly towards me. Harm in the form of a slapping hand. I shouted in fear and the schoolmaster shouted in anger. Iqbal just shouted for me to get out. So I ran to the door with Iqbal behind me. Iqbal was pushing hard against my back. Luckily the schoolmaster does not allow the shoes indoors or else he would have taken his shoe and thrown it at my round head. That would have been a bad scene. Being hit by shoes is like covering injury with insult.

So now we were out on the road once again. The rain was gone, which was good because I had left my black umbrella at the schoolmaster's flat. And now it was impossible to return to claim it. Doing so would only alert the schoolmaster to the availability of a weapon for use on my perfectly bulbous round head or stomach.

I was pleased to be outside and safe on the dry Mumbai roads. Actually wet roads, but soon to be dry because of stoppage of rain and startage of sun. But quickly my pleasure became displeasure when I caught sight of Iqbal's worried face. I told him not to worry. The schoolmaster only wanted to harm me, not him. His relation with the schoolmaster will be unaffected.

Iqbal said no, that is not my worry. My worry is the original problem. Onion problem.

I said no, that can no longer be the major worry. Now we are in a pursuit situation, and all else must become secondary. Is that not the commitment we have made as Gandhians?

Iqbal nodded his head as if to say yes.

Then I reminded him that did Gandhiji not say that all other problems will be solved as a byproduct of a sincere pursuit of the truth?

Iqbal nodded his head and even may have said yes quietly.

So, I said, we must continue our aggressive pursuit of the truth, and your original onion problem will be solved as a byproduct. Is that not logical?

Now Iqbal nodded his head and said yes loudly.

I smiled with satisfaction at my own powers of persuasiveness. I put my arm around my brother and pointed up to the sky. So, I said, our next step is to perform a comparison amongst imperfect vegetables to determine how to increase surface area devoted to onion production.

But then when I said those words my smile disappeared because I remembered that I did not know the answer. Actually the schoolmaster is correct. Although I am quite smart in some areas, like maths, in other things I am quite a stupid bugger.

Iqbal sensed my anxiousness and calmed me down. He said not to worry, we will seek the advice of a specialist on the vegetable comparison.

But how, I said. The vegetablewalla said we are bastards, so we cannot ask him.

Iqbal said no, the vegetablewalla may sell vegetables, but he is not a specialist in the use of vegetables. We must go to the person who makes crucial decisions involving vegetables. The man whose very life and existence depends on accurate judgments regarding the suitability of one vegetable over another.

Yes, yes, I said. But who is this person?

Now Iqbal smiled and raised his finger. The pao-bhaji-walla, he said.

Even I smiled now. Yes, yes, I said. That is an excellent plan. Let us go to the pao-bhaji-walla.

Actually I did not completely follow Iqbal's plan, but I like pao-bhaji and so I was happy. Plus, it was almost two hours before lunchtime and so I was quite hungry already.

5

For those of you that have not been to Mumbai and are therefore unfamiliar with the wondrousness of pao-bhaji, allow me to explain. Pao-bhaji is a wondrous thing. It is a combination of a simple thing and a complicated thing, and the result is wondrous in its simple complexity. The simple thing is the pao. Pao means bread. A simple bun of soft and fluffy white baker's bread. The complicated thing is the bhaji. The complexity of bhaji begins with the name itself. It can mean many things. In the north, like in Punjab, they call each other bhaji like how I call Iqbal brother. In Mumbai we don't say such things. How silly it would be if I introduced Iqbal as my bhaji in life? Silly, isn't it? Iqbal is nodding now. He agrees that it would be silly to call him bhaji.

But the other meaning of bhaji is a mixture of vegetables. And this is the meaning taken by the word that combines with pao to create the wondrous pao-bhaji. So now it is clearer to me, and to you also I hope, why the pao-bhaji-walla is a specialist in comparison of vegetables. After all, he mixes all the different vegetables in the precise combination to provide this wondrous creation that is eaten far and wide in this greatest city of Mumbai.

So in short time we arrived at the post of the pao-bhaji-walla. He occupies a position at the front of the lane, at the exact intersection point of our lane and the main road. This is prime territory for him, because this way he gets all the regular traffic from the lane as well as casual customers from the main road. Of course, me and Iqbal are regular, not casual. Actually I am quite a serious customer. Not casual at all.

So we stood and watched the pao-bhaji-walla as his helper served the few casual customers that had placed orders and were standing around his open-air stall. The pao-bhaji-walla was in his usual white vest and was facing a massive open pan on which the bhaji was cooking. He was mixing the bhaji with his steel spatula in a perfect timed motion: *tuk-tuk-tuk, tuk-tuk-tuk, tuk-tuk-tuk.*

It was a sight of absolute synchronized bliss. Complete proof of the mathematical precision that underlies the universe. I looked at Iqbal and smiled. He too understood the perfection implied by the pao-bhaji-walla mashing and pushing and pulling the bhaji across the big flat round open pan.

Tuk-tuk-tuk, tuk-tuk-tuk, tuk-tuk-tuk.

We waited and watched as the other customers ate their fill and drank their juice. We smiled as the customers touched their heavy stomachs and nodded their approvals. Yes, the pao-bhaji-walla was definitely the person who could explain how to compare the vegetables.

But first we ordered two plates of pao-bhaji from him, of which I myself ate one-and-half plates. Each plate comes with two breads, and I finished total three breads. See, I am quite good at maths, as I said. I am also good at philosophical questions. Not so good at answers though. It is Iqbal, my brother in life, that is the answer-man.

So we finished our pao-bhaji and drank our juice and waited until the helper had taken our plates and glasses to the bucket of water that contained the other plates and glasses. Then we looked at each other and looked at the pao-bhaji-walla. Iqbal gave me a look that meant I should do the asking. I was nervous, but I understood that since I am the more serious customer, it is logical that I ask the first question. So I rubbed my bulbous head for good luck and went ahead. I asked him the big question.

Bhaiyya, how you can make such judgments of the relative value of onion versus other vegetables, I asked him.

The pao-bhaji-walla looked at me but he did not say a word. He simply continued with his mixing motion: *tuk-tuk-tuk, tuk-tuk-tuk, tuk-tuk-tuk.*

I was little taken aback at this point. After all, I was quite a serious customer. Not casual at all. Perhaps the pao-bhaji-walla did not hear me over the noise of his mixing. So I asked him once again.

The pao-bhaji-walla looked at me again and still he did not say a word. But this time he gave a small smile. Very small smile, almost too small to notice. But I noticed. I am very observant. I thought he would answer now, but he did not. He simply mixed the vegetables: *tuk-tuk-tuk, tuk-tuk-tuk, tuk-tuk-tuk.*

Now I was unsure whether to be annoyed or scared. This pursuit of truth was not going as fast as imagined. I turned and looked to Iqbal for some guidance. Iqbal is the answer-man, after all. Iqbal simply made a gesture that indicated I should ask once more. So I asked yet again.

This time the pao-bhaji-walla looked at me and then he did one more round of mixing and suddenly stopped mixing his vegetables with a loud last *TUK*. He held out his hand and the helper gave him a small towel. The pao-bhaji-walla mopped the sweat from his face and arms and neck. Then he looked at me and smiled.

RK-sahib, you have eaten well, no? he asked me.

Yes of course, I said.

Sure? All is fine at home? he asked.

Yes, yes. Very much so.

Then why you ask me to tell you how I make my bhaji?

Now I understood. No, no, I said. I do not want your recipe. I only want explanation of how you decide on your recipe.

The pao-bhaji-walla closed one eye and looked at me with the other eye. Smart man you are, he said. You do not want my recipe, but you want to know how I created my recipe?

No, no, I said. See, the situation is this—

I see nothing, he said. Situation or not, I do not care. These are my secrets. I am a businessman, you know.

I became quite worried now. The pao-bhaji-walla looked

angry, and his helper looked very scared. Then suddenly I became scared also. What if the pao-bhaji-walla puts me on the black list? Actually I do not know if he even has a black list. He is a roadside vendor, after all. He cannot read or write. Still, as a serious customer, I was quite concerned.

Iqbal, my brother in life, sensed my high degree of concern and stepped into the situation. He put his hand on my shoulder to indicate that I should not speak for little while. Then he smiled at the pao-bhaji-walla.

Bhaiyya, he said, RK and I are Gandhians, and we are in the pursuit of truth.

Truth of what, the pao-bhaji-walla asked. Truth about the universe? Life? God? Death? Love?

Pao-bhaji-walla was serious. After all, this is India. All kinds of people are running around searching for truth in all these high-funda matters. And many of these people talk about such things when standing near roadside pao-bhaji stalls.

Iqbal laughed and said no, we only want truth about onion problem.

Now the pao-bhaji-walla made a very serious face. Yes, he said, I have heard about onion problem.

Now Iqbal became anxious. What have you heard, he said.

Pao-bhaji-walla was quiet. Then he spoke, but quietly. First you tell me what you have heard, he said.

Iqbal looked at me and then back at the pao-bhaji-walla. I have heard that onion prices have become very high. This is because of simple case of supply and demand. But supply and demand is quite complex, actually. See, demand only increases because of Mumbaikar population increase, while supply may increase or decrease depending on many factors.

Such as onion supply decrease because of encroachment by China on our borders, I said. Iqbal looked at me as if to say shut up. The pao-bhaji-walla looked at me like I was mad. I shut up immediately. Let Iqbal speak, I thought.

Iqbal continued to speak. See, he said, if demand increases, then the only way to stop price from increasing is to also increase supply of onion. And there is only one feasible way to do so.

The pao-bhaji-walla was looking very interested. Even his helper was listening with great interest.

Iqbal was speaking louder now. So, he said, the one way is to increase surface area used for onion production by reducing surface area used for production of other vegetables. And therefore we must understand how to pass judgment on which vegetable is inferior to onion. In this way we can find the truth about how to increase onion supply and maintain stable onion price, which will solve the onion problem. And we know that since you are mixing the vegetables daily with great precision and perfection, you would know how to pass judgment on which vegetable is more or less important than onion.

The pao-bhaji-walla nodded his head as if to say yes, he understands. Then he shook his head as if to say no, he cannot help us. See, he said, it is impossible for me to pass such judgment.

But why, said Iqbal.

Because this judgment cannot be made. My bhaji is different from all other bhajis. The pao-bhaji stall in the next lane uses a different proportion of onion in the bhaji. And that is different from what you will get when you order pao-bhaji at a proper restaurant or hotel. And that will be different from my bhaji also. So for me to pass judgment on basis of all bhajis is not correct. It is quite impossible. No, I cannot answer your question. You will have to look elsewhere.

But you must know something about this, said Iqbal. After all, you are a master of mixing vegetables. You know which vegetables are more useful and which are less useful.

No, it is not possible to say, said the pao-bhaji-walla. Some vegetables may be used in small quantities by me but in large quantities for other bhajis. And although I know my own bhaji is superior, I have come to accept that some people prefer other bhajis to mine.

But there must be some vegetable that is used in small quantities in all bhajis, I said. Surely this vegetable is less useful than onion. So please tell us the name of that vegetable and then that will be the answer.

The pao-bhaji-walla looked at me like I was mad. You are a stupid bugger, he said. Even after all your schooling you are a stupid bugger.

I was quite angry now. How everyone can call me a stupid bugger, I do not understand. But I held my tongue and touched my round head and suffered in silence for the sake of the truth.

The pao-bhaji-walla continued. Quantity of vegetable has no bearing on usefulness of vegetable, he said. I may use a small amount of chillies and large amounts of tomatoes, but no one can say that the chillies are less useful than the tomato.

Then the tomato is less useful than the chilli, I said. There, that must be the answer. That is logical. If the chilli is not less useful than the tomato, then it must be more useful, and therefore the tomato is less useful. So that is the answer. Tomato is the most useless vegetable, and so we can safely reduce tomato production and increase onion production, thereby solving the onion problem. See, I am not such a stupid bugger after all.

The pao-bhaji-walla shook his head and laughed in my face. No, he said, you are not a stupid bugger after all. Actually you are a stupid bastard. Not bugger, but bastard.

Now his helper laughed at me also, and I lost my temper. I reached out to slap the helper, but Iqbal pushed my hand away, and in doing so I lost my balance and fell sideways. I fell onto the bucket that held the dirty plates, and immediately the bucket broke and all the plates fell to the pavement. Of course, the plates were all stainless steel so they did not break, but the bucket was quite broken.

So immediately me and Iqbal ran from there.

6

We ran onto the main road and into another lane some distance away from our lane. When we stopped running, we looked around and noticed that it was a lane to which we had not been in the past. This was quite unusual, because Iqbal and me are quite familiar with our neighboring lanes.

The lane was not even a proper lane. Proper lanes have exits on both ends, but this lane was a dead-end. In fact it was more like a courtyard than a lane. Perhaps that is why we had not been here prior to this occasion. We decided to stand there for little time. Let the pao-bhaji-walla and his helper forget about us and then we may venture back to our lane. So we stood there, me and Iqbal, my brother in life.

Presently I felt something at the back of my feet, and then we heard a voice. The voice was politely asking us to move our feet. We turned, and in turning we noticed that the voice came from a sweeper. By sweeper I mean the fellow who sweeps the street with a broom.

This sweeper was quite young. Much younger than us, but perhaps older than our children, all of whom were approximately college age. He was clean shaven and he wore spectacles.

It was not a problem for us to move, so we both moved and allowed the sweeper to continue with his work. After all, who are we to stop a young sweeper from doing his work? Besides, we had bigger problems. Our so-called expert in vegetable comparison turned out to give us no good answer.

I complained to Iqbal about the situation. This pursuit of truth, I said, is not so easy. In fact it has already caused us lot of problems. First with the schoolmaster, and now with the pao-bhaji-walla. And I do not like how all these people are calling me stupid bugger and what-not.

Iqbal said I should calm down.

I said what calm down? This is getting too much. We should have just downgraded the word from pursuit to acceptance. Then we would be home right now and drinking tea on my balcony and watching the rain.

Iqbal said no, that is not true. Firstly, it is not raining. And secondly, maybe you would have been home drinking tea, but I would still have the onion problem to take care of.

I felt bad now and said sorry.

Iqbal said don't worry. No need for sorry. Remember, when I was thinking it was too much, you encouraged me and said that all problems will be solved as byproduct of pursuing the truth. So now I must encourage you in return. It is only right. We are brothers in life, after all.

I felt much better now. Little bit encouraged even. I smiled and nodded. Okay then, I said. What next?

Iqbal looked at the ground. He did not know.

I too was not sure. Maybe we simply ask a different pao-bhaji-walla, I said.

No use, Iqbal said. They will all say the same thing. More chillies here, less tomatoes here, extra turmeric here, and so on and so forth. We will simply create more confusion and more trouble.

Yes, Iqbal was right. Plus, I did not want any more trouble with pao-bhaji-wallas. It could result in some inconvenience for my own pao-bhaji consumption. Then again I felt something at the back of my feet and I turned and again it was the sweeper. This time I got little annoyed.

Why are you sweeping at our feet when the entire courtyard is there for you to sweep? I asked the sweeper.

The sweeper looked at me through his spectacles and smiled. Why are you standing where I must sweep when the entire courtyard is there for you to stand? he said.

That is not the point, I said. We are standing here, so you must sweep here only after we move.

The sweeper shook his head. Who are you to say that standing takes priority over sweeping? he said. In fact, it may even be the other way around.

No, I said. It cannot be that way. If that were the case, then everywhere there would be sweeping and nowhere would there be standing.

The sweeper laughed. That makes no sense, he said. You are quite a silly bugger.

I was getting increasingly irritated. If he had called me a stupid bugger or a silly bastard then I would have slapped him definitely. But since he only said silly bugger, I waited. Soon he would say something silly, and then I would slap this bugger.

Now Iqbal put his hand on my shoulder again to calm me. I became calm.

The sweeper smiled at me. Sorry, he said. I did not mean to make you upset. I only want to do my work properly. Actually I have finished sweeping elsewhere. Only this place is still dirty, and that is why I am sweeping at your feet.

Now I felt little sorry. I said I too am sorry. Me and Iqbal, my brother in life, are engaged in a very important question for which we have found no answer, and so I was already little upset to begin with. Sorry, I said again.

What is the question, the sweeper asked.

I explained about the onion problem and the resulting question of how to pass judgment on the vegetables and then how the pao-bhaji-walla had said judgment is not passable. I did not mention the breakages of the schoolmaster's tea set and the pao-bhaji-walla's bucket.

So what is the problem, the sweeper asked.

Funny man you are, I said. The problem is apparent. How are we to pass judgment on the relative value of vegetables if judgment is not passable?

I do not see any apparent problem, the sweeper said, because it is a stupid matter that you are worried about.

How can it be stupid? I said. It is an answer that is required for the further pursuit of the truth and the ultimate resolution of the onion problem.

It is a pointless question, said the sweeper. What action will you take if you get an answer to your stupid pointless question?

I was confused. I looked at Iqbal. He remained quiet.

The sweeper leaned on his tall broom handle. See, he said. Let us say the answer is that tomato is less important than onion. In that case, what will you do? What action will you take? How will you reduce the tomato crop and increase onion crop? You think you will run around and tell farmers to replace tomato land with onion plantations? And even if you do, you think they will listen to a silly bugger like you?

I was about to reply in haste but then Iqbal piped in.

No, he said. We have no action plan.

Then it is a pointless question, said the sweeper. If you have no action planned with the answer, then what use is the answer?

But it is the truth, I said. The truth has its own plan. It is a plan in itself. That is the teaching of Gandhiji. And we are Gandhians.

The sweeper shook his head. No, he said. If there is no action, then the truth is useless, which means there is no truth. Just like if I do not sweep, the street will not get clean.

I was quite confused now, but Iqbal was nodding his head, so I kept quiet. Maybe Iqbal understood what this bugger was saying. I would ask Iqbal later. I did not want to embarrass myself in front of a sweeper.

The sweeper looked at me. Do you understand, he said.

Now I was forced to answer. Of course, I said.

What is your understanding, the sweeper said.

I breathed deeply before speaking. Then I spoke. You mean the truth is like the broom, I said. It is meaningless if not used to clean the dirty street. And so we must first find the dirty street to clean, and only then should we worry about the broom.

Iqbal looked at me in silence.

The sweeper also stared at me for some time. Then he smiled. You are a funny bugger, he said. Go on, move your feet so I can sweep.

7

The sweeper left us in peace after that. We stood quietly for some more time, then we carefully looked out onto the main road to see if the pao-bhaji-walla or his helper were keeping watch for us. It looked clear, so we moved out of the courtyard.

By now it was getting quite hot, so I looked around for some shelter. I saw that a local bank was open, and I could see through the glass walls that there was a long line of people standing in front of the teller windows.

Ah good, I said. The bank is quite busy. Let us go sit in the air-conditioned waiting area. We can safely pass some time there in the cool air without any trouble.

Iqbal gave me a look, but then he also looked at the sun and finally said okay.

So we walked into the air-conditioned bank and sat on two chairs in the waiting area.

We must think of a possible action, I said. A possible action that will advance us on the path of the pursuit of truth.

Yes, said Iqbal, but the sweeper was correct. We have no plan to adjust crop plantation patterns. So the question of passing judgment amongst vegetables is definitely pointless.

Then what question can we ask in pursuit of the solution? I said this loudly, and the man sitting next to us in the waiting area made a face at me like I was talking too loudly.

Iqbal pulled on his beard like he does when he is thinking. We must take one step in reverse, he said. We must keep going in reverse until we find a solution that can be acted upon by us.

I did not follow, and I said so.

Iqbal explained. See, he said, the schoolmaster said that two possible options are there for increase of land area devoted to onion production. One is to replace other crops with onion crops. And the other is to find more available land.

Now I understood. Okay, I said, and since we have no action plan even if we can pass judgment on vegetables, we must therefore discard that option and pursue the truth along the path of the other option.

Iqbal smiled and nodded his head while still touching his beard.

I too was happy at my fine display of logical process. But then quickly the happiness disappeared when I remembered the words of the schoolmaster. I reminded Iqbal of this.

You are right, said Iqbal, the schoolmaster did in fact tell us that not much unused land is available for onion production.

Yes, I said. So we must revert to the previous option. I spoke the next words loudly, because I was proud. After all, it was myself who had suggested the previous option. The option to reclaim land from Bangladesh, Pakistan, and China. So I proclaimed this loudly.

When I did so, the entire waiting room turned to look at me. I was still quite proud, but then Iqbal tapped me on the shoulder and said that if we make noise, we may be thrown from the bank. After all, he said, we are not bank customers.

I agreed, and I kept quiet for some time. After some more time I noticed that the man sitting next to me was still staring at me even though the other customers were minding their own businesses. At first it was a look that I recognized—the same look that other people gave me just before calling me a stupid bugger or silly bastard or some other pornographic name. But now it was a different look, a look like he was thinking about something involving me. Not pornographic involvement of course, but schematic involvement. By that I mean he was thinking of some scheme involving me.

So I waited for him to say something, and presently he did exactly that.

You are interested in reclaiming land from Pakistan and Bangladesh and China? he asked me.

Perhaps, I said.

Then you must be a true patriot, he said.

Perhaps, I said.

The man shook his head quite violently. Not perhaps, but definitely, he said.

Okay, I said, definitely then.

You are Bose-ian? he said.

I said no, Gandhi-ian.

Then your statements are contradictory, he said.

No no, of course not, I said. Then I thought for one minute. What statements? I asked.

That you want to reclaim land from Pakistan and Bangladesh and China.

How contradictory? There is no contradiction.

But of course.

No. How?

Because Gandhi himself was the cause of the delivery of land to Pakistan and Bangladesh and China.

No no, I said. Pakistan was created by Jinnah and the British. In fact, Gandhi was against it. He wanted to make Jinnah the first prime minister, but it was not allowed. And then both the Indo-China war as well as the creation of Bangladesh were post-Bapu. So how could Gandhi have delivered land to China and Bangladesh after his death?

Never mind all that, said the man. That is all history. It does not matter now.

Funny man you are, I said. Just now you're saying that Gandhiji did this and Gandhiji did that. If that is not history, then what else is it? You are talking about history only. Without history, this conversation makes no sense. And remember the saying, I said, those who do not remember history will forget it.

The man was quiet for one or two minutes. Then he spoke again. That is not the saying, he said. The saying is this: those who remember too much history will keep doing the same things again and again like stupid buggers. Therefore it is best to leave history alone.

Now I was quiet. Some logic was there in his statements, yes.

Do you see my logic, the man said.

Perhaps, I said.

Okay then. Listen to me now. Based on your previously uttered statements, I believe you are a man of action, yes?

I immediately became very happy. Action, I thought, is exactly what we are in search of at this point.

Yes, I said. Very much so. Without action, there is no truth. Just like how without the broom there is no dirty street.

The man looked at me in that earlier way for just a moment. First I thought he was going to call me some names, but then he simply laughed.

I am a member of a group, he said. A group of men of action. And one or two women of action also, but mostly men for now. We are having trouble recruiting females at this point.

What is this group, I said. I was getting interested. The talk of action was making me active. Either that or the pao-bhaji was creating action in my stomach.

It is a Bose-ian group, he said.

You mean it is followers of Netaji? I asked.

The man smiled. Indeed, he said, we are disciples of Netaji Subhash Chandra Bose.

I nodded in respect. He was a great leader, I said. It is unfortunate that he disappeared during the World War Two action. I shook my head in further respect. He died in a plane crash over Taiwan area, I said, that is the rumor.

The man stopped smiling. He moved close to me. Then he moved even closer until his mouth was close to my ear.

No, he said.

No means what? I asked. I was quite uncomfortable with this extreme closeness.

Netaji is with us, he said.

I nodded in respect. Yes, I said, and Bapu as well as the other great freedom fighters. They will always be with us.

No, no, he said. I mean with us in real form, not spiritual form.

I stared at him like he was a madman, which he probably might be.

How can you say such things, I asked. It is impossible.

How can it be impossible when it is true? the man said.

That sounded logical. If it was true, then it could not be impossible. I thought for one or two minutes. Then I spoke. What proof do you have of Netaji being here in real form? I said.

He smiled. I have all the proof that is needed for my satisfaction, he said.

What is that proof? How are you sure that Netaji is alive today? I asked.

Because, the man said, I know him personally and very well. Come, I will take you to him and you will see the proof for yourself.

8

So now we stood once more in the street. Me, Iqbal, and this madman who promised to take us to Netaji, the great Indian freedom fighter who is rumored to have disappeared in the skies above Taiwan in 1945. Or more precisely, in the ashes of the plane that was destroyed in Taiwanese region in 1945. Of course, the body was never recovered, and there is always some madman who says Netaji is alive somewhere. I just did not think I would actually meet such a madman.

Come, said the man, it is close by. He will be done with his morning routine, and will be free to see us before lunchtime.

I thought about lunchtime and felt quite happy, so I followed him. I looked at Iqbal, who was also following, but more slowly. Iqbal gave me a look that meant be careful, we are following a madman. I smiled at Iqbal, my brother in life.

The madman led us back down the main road quite fast. Then suddenly he turned left and we followed him and immediately found ourselves in the very same courtyard where we had previously been hiding. I looked back at Iqbal in surprise, and I could tell that he too was surprised.

There he is, said the madman. He is just finishing. Let us wait.

Where? I said. I looked around but I could see no one, just the sweeper.

There, said the madman. He pointed to the sweeper.

You are a real madman, I said. I should slap you right here and now.

9

Of course I did not slap the madman. I was a Gandhian, after all. As I said, nonviolence is part and parcel of being Gandhian. Besides, we were on an active pursuit of truth, and we were now taking action towards that pursuit. So, in the interest of truth, we must follow through on what this madman was saying.

The madman smiled and folded his hands and said namaste and bowed to the sweeper. The sweeper gestured to him to indicate that bowing was not required. Then the sweeper looked at us and smiled.

Ah, my silly Gandhian friends, he said. We meet again.

I was not sure what to say. I turned to Iqbal, but he gave me a look that meant it is your problem to talk to these madmen. So I turned back to the sweeper.

Yes, I said.

I cautiously looked at the madman. He was still bowing slightly.

Now the sweeper looked at the madman and smiled. Why have you brought these Gandhians to me, Bhatkoo? he said to the madman.

Netaji, I met them at the bank when I was making the weekly deposit, said the madman whose name I surmised was Bhatkoo. Funny name, but appropriate for a madman.

They were speaking of reclaiming land from China and Pakistan and Bangladesh, and so I thought they are men of action like yourself and like all of us, said Bhatkoo. He smiled very widely. Bhatkoo was very pleased with his work, it seemed.

I see, said the sweeper. He looked at me. So, you are a man of action now, is it?

Yes, I proclaimed.

Okay, good. We can use such men in our group, said the sweeper.

I was not sure how to ask the sweeper the burning question. I looked at Iqbal. He shook his head as an indication that I must ask the question. So I did.

Tell me one thing, I said, your madman, I mean your man Bhatkoo, has said some impossible things about you.

Like what? said the sweeper.

I hesitated. It is hard for me to say, I told him. It is not a serious thing.

Go ahead, the sweeper said, I like jokes.

Never mind, I said. It is not a good joke.

Netaji, they are doubting that you are Netaji, said Bhatkoo.

The sweeper turned to me with an angry look. What is there to doubt? he said. Why should we lie about such things?

I was not sure how to engage with such foolish conversation. But I did so anyway. First of all, I said, you are younger than myself, and only barely older than my children, all of whom are in college.

That is only in appearance, said the sweeper. My college days were long time back. I was at Cambridge around 1920. And Presidency College in Calcutta before that. He smiled. Those were fine years.

I stared at this young man who had no wrinkles on his skin talk about being in college about ninety years earlier. I did some mental calculations, and even though I did not know the official birth year of Netaji Subhash Chandra Bose, my calculations placed his age at around one hundred and ten years. Impossible. These are bloody madmen, I thought.

So I smiled at the young man and then I turned to Iqbal and gave him a look that meant come, let us quickly run away from these mad buggers. But to my surprise, Iqbal stepped forward and began talking.

How come you have no wrinkles if you are hundred-plus years in age, said Iqbal. I was impressed that Iqbal had also done the mental maths.

The sweeper laughed. You want my secrets to a youthful appearance? he said. It is too soon to give away such valuable information.

Now it was time for me to be the voice of sense and calmness and reason. I grabbed Iqbal's arm and said come on, let us get away from the madmen.

But Iqbal pushed away my grip and gave me a look of determination and resolve. This is a test, he said. This is the ultimate test of whether we are truly willing to pursue the truth wherever he or she may lie.

It, I said.

What? said Iqbal.

It. We decided that the truth was genderless, I said.

Iqbal did not respond. For one second I thought he would slap me for changing the topic by introducing such a trivial matter when issues of immense gravity are at stake.

Okay fine, I said. We can do little more pursuit.

The sweeper was watching all this with amusement. Bhatkoo was also smiling at our display.

Now the sweeper came forward. Okay, he said. I will say one or two things about my youthful appearance. But then you must promise to spend little more time with me to learn about our activities and perhaps join our group.

I thought for one minute. As long as it is in the interest of learning and pursuit of the truth, I said.

Of course, the sweeper said. It is all in the interest of wisdom and truth. Without those things, what else is there?

Action, I said. Action is also there.

Yes, said the sweeper. I only told you that on your previous visit to my courtyard.

Oh, yes, I said.

Funny bugger you are, he said.

Sorry, I said.

No need for sorry. Funny buggers are always welcome in my courtyard, he said.

You are the owner of this courtyard? I asked.

Yes, he said. Of course. Is it not obvious?

I looked around at the courtyard. It was not obvious to me, but then I am not so smart in some non-mathematical things.

Why you sweep your own courtyard? I asked. Netaji would never sweep his own courtyard.

It seems you know nothing about what Netaji would or would not do, he said. After all, I am Netaji, and I am sweeping my own courtyard, so is that not proof that you do not know what Netaji would or would not do?

I thought about it. His statement seemed logical in appearance, but smelled little off. Still, I could not find the source of the smell, so I let it go for now.

Iqbal was not paying attention. He was still looking at the sweeper's face. What about the wrinkles? he said.

Now the sweeper put on a serious face. Okay, he said. I will explain how to prevent wrinkles.

Iqbal moved closer, and so did I.

First, said the sweeper, you must minimize sun exposure.

But you are a sweeper, I said. How can you minimize sun exposure when you are sweeping in the sun every day?

The sweeper shook his head. No, he said. I usually finish before the sun rises. But today due to the unseasonal rain, I had to sweep later. So today is an exception. Few exceptions are allowed. It creates some variety, which is also good for the skin.

Okay, I said.

What else? said Iqbal.

Number two, said the sweeper, is that you must always lie on your back when you sleep. No sleeping on your side, and no sleeping on your stomach. You must lie with your face looking directly up at the ceiling.

Impossible, I said. Absolutely impossible.

Iqbal also looked dubious.

The sweeper smiled. It cannot be impossible if I accomplish it every day. And since I accomplish it every day, it is not impossible. Is that not logical?

I nodded. It sounded logical.

But how? said Iqbal.

I have some people from my group tie me to my bed in the appropriate position, said the sweeper. Once I am secured, I cannot move to either side, and so the sleeping posture is easily accomplished.

Iqbal nodded. Okay, he said, I understand. One must be secured with rope in bed.

What else, I said.

There is one more thing, said the sweeper. But it is not a simple thing to explain.

But you must explain, I said. We must have the truth. It is our duty, our obligation.

The sweeper was quiet. Then he shook his head. No, he said, it is not a simple thing. It is quite complex, actually. I do not think you Gandhians are ready for such truths.

Nonsense, I said. Gandhians by definition are making constant preparations for truths of any kind and any gender.

The sweeper looked little confused at my last comment, but he did not say anything. He seemed to be thinking. Then he spoke. Okay, he said, I will say the third thing.

Okay, wonderful, I said.

The third condition for preventing wrinkles, he said, is to avoid all worry.

Now I laughed. He really was a madman.

Even Iqbal laughed. You are a madman, he said. I was surprised, because Iqbal does not call people such names.

See, the sweeper said. It is not a simple thing. You are not capable of understanding.

Now I became curious. No, no, I said. We are definitely capable. You must explain it little more though. You cannot just say to avoid worry.

Okay, said the sweeper. But you must come inside the building with me. I cannot explain it here. It is too sunny.

10

And so our pursuit of truth took us deeper into the world of the madmen. But nobody said pursuing the truth would involve only sane people. Besides, if this madman who says he is Netaji tells us how to avoid worry, then it will not matter whether he is Netaji or simply a madman. The truth will be independent of his mental status or birth certificate.

The interior of the building attached to the courtyard was extremely curious. The main hall was quite dark to begin with, which was strange because there were many windows, all of which were facing the blast of the Mumbai sun. And the Mumbai sun can deliver quite a blast, I tell you.

I was going to ask Netaji about this curious darkness, but I held back. I did not want to distract him or annoy him. After all, if these are madmen, who is to say what will set them off?

It is a special unidirectional tinted glass, said Netaji.

What? I said.

Yes, said Bhatkoo, it has been developed by one of the scientists in our group.

Netaji nodded. Also helpful in preventing sun exposure when indoors, he said.

Okay, I said, okay then.

Nice one, said Iqbal.

Netaji smiled. Yes, he said, we have some useful people in our group.

Now I became more curious about his group. First I had thought they would all be madmen, but perhaps there was more to it. After all, this one-way tinted glass was quite a fancy invention, and definitely not a creation of madmen. So I looked at Iqbal, who nodded in approval. And then I proceeded with a question.

Netaji, I said, tell us one or two things about this group.

Netaji looked at me. His eyebrow was raised, and I felt little uncomfortable, like I was asking something that should not be asked.

Perhaps, said Netaji. Perhaps I will say one or two things.

Then he was quiet. He walked deeper into the interior of the building and we quietly followed him. Presently I noticed that Bhatkoo had somehow disappeared, and now only the three of us were present. I was not sure whether to be worried, and so I decided not to worry.

There is no need to worry, said Netaji, even though it is dark and getting darker.

No problem, I said, we are not worried.

Okay good, said Netaji, because it would be needless to worry.

Okay good, I said.

But internally I was wondering if I should get little worried. After all, it was dark and getting darker, and we were following a madman into this dark place. I looked behind me to see if Iqbal was following. I saw his outline and white kurta, but I could not read his expression due to the darkness. I became little worried, and I thought about my wife. And then immediately I thought about food.

Will there be any food where we are going? I said.

Although I could not see, I could feel Iqbal's look. Undoubtedly he was giving me a look for speaking of food at a serious time like this. I felt bad, but what to do?

Netaji laughed. Of course, he said, but it will be vegetarian food only.

No problem, I said.

You are vegetarian? Iqbal asked.

Not always, said Netaji. No, sometimes I like to eat good fish. But Mumbai has no good fish. Not like we used to get in Bengal.

Yes, I understand, Iqbal said. You Bengalis like to eat the fish from rivers. Here we eat fish from open seas and oceans. So there is a difference.

Big difference, said Netaji.

Not so much I think, said Iqbal.

I tried to send Iqbal a look that said don't argue with the madman in the darkness, but the look could not be conveyed due to said darkness. So I let the argument about fish proceed.

Very big difference, said Netaji. These Mumbai fish have not much taste. Especially that pomfret creature.

Okay yes, said Iqbal. That much is true. But the Bombay-duck is a tasty fish.

Ah, okay fine, said Netaji. Bombay-duck is fine enough. I eat it sometimes, especially when it is double-fried with extra turmeric and double-extra salt.

I myself do not like Bombay-duck so much. It is a skinny and bony fish and I have to eat at least fifteen to twenty of the buggers to feel full.

Still, since Iqbal and Netaji were in agreement, I did not want to add any disturbance to the situation.

Yes, I said, you are both correct.

You also like Bombay-duck? Netaji asked me.

Now I was not sure how to reply. It did not seem good to lie whilst in active pursuit of the truth. But I did not want to get into an argument in the darkness with a potential madman. So I tried to evade the subject.

I am from Bombay, I said, and I love all things about Bombay.

Rubbish, said Netaji. You are either blind or you are a liar. Now which is it, he asked me, blind or liar?

Now I was really in trouble. I thought for a minute, and then, by taking the increasing darkness into account, I replied confidently.

Blind, I said.

Okay, said Netaji. Then I will help you along the path to visibility. First I will have my people bring some Bombay-ducks. And we will have them double-fried with turmeric.

And double-extra salt, said Iqbal.

Iqbal seemed very excited, and this only made me angry. Not only was I angry at Iqbal, but also at myself. My own lies had put me in a position where I would be forced to eat this fish that I did not prefer. I made a sound and kept walking.

But of course, said Netaji, there will also be some onion bhajias.

My ears and tongue perked up at the mention of bhajias, which are lovely deep-fried fritters of vegetables covered in chickpea batter. Ah, good. Now I only hoped that Iqbal would not speak of the onion problem.

So, your group has not been affected by onion problem, is it? asked Iqbal.

If there had been more light, I would definitely have slapped Iqbal. Who gives a bloody damn about onion problems when bhajias are at stake?

There is no onion problem here, said Netaji.

Not yet, but soon there might be, said Iqbal. It is coming. It is a simple case of supply and demand, you see.

Yes, yes, said Netaji. You both explained this to me earlier. But see, there is no onion problem here.

How can that be? Iqbal said.

Because we manage our demand and supply from within the group itself, said Netaji.

Means what? I said.

You silly bugger, said Netaji, it simply means we eat the onions that we grow, and we grow the onions that we eat.

Your group owns onion farmland? asked Iqbal.

Netaji laughed. You might say that. You will see for yourself soon enough. We are almost there now.

But it is only getting darker here, I said. It appears we are moving more to the interior than the exterior. How can there be farmland in the building?

No land is necessary, said Netaji. It is a simple matter of hydroponics.

Means what? I said.

Means growth of plant without land. Only water is necessary, said Netaji.

Amazing, I said. Your scientists must be very smart.

No, said Netaji. It is the onion that is smart. Our scientists have not invented hydroponics. In fact, the plants only have invented it.

Absolute nonsense, I said. A plant cannot invent anything. It is a stupid creature.

Quiet, said Netaji. He stopped immediately and turned to me. Do not say such things, he said. The plants may hear you, and then we may have a real onion problem.

I laughed. Plants cannot hear, I said, you are the stupid bugger now. I laughed again.

And then Netaji slapped me quite hard and I shouted.

Netaji made two or three sounds in Bengali, and suddenly out of the darkness came Bhatkoo and two or three other people. They grabbed on to me and Iqbal, some of them pulling, and some of them pushing, but all of them grabbing. And before we knew it the darkness had become light and we were pushed and pulled and grabbed until we found ourselves thrown back out into the courtyard. That very same courtyard in which we had started. But now we were alone, with no bhajias, no Bombay-ducks, and no truth.

II

We stood in silence for some time, and then I took Iqbal to task.

Why must you open your small little mouth, you fool? I said to him. If you had not mentioned onion problem, then we would right now be eating onion bhajias and learning the truth about how to avoid wrinkles by eliminating worry from life.

Iqbal kept his mouth shut. He was staring at the dark windows of the building from which we had been expelled.

What are you staring at, you stupid bugger? I said to Iqbal.

Iqbal did not respond. Instead of responding, he continued to stare at the windows. At one window, to be precise.

Presently Iqbal turned to me and smiled. Look, he said.

I don't want to look at anything, I said, because I am angry and because I am hungry.

Now look, I tell you, said Iqbal.

His voice was loud, which is uncommon for Iqbal, and so I looked at where he was pointing. I could now see why he was smiling.

In the one dark window, I could see one dark figure. The figure was holding a torch. I mean a torch that has batteries, not the one with flames. The torch was moving, and it seemed to be a signal. Of course, I could not understand this signal, so I looked at Iqbal, my brother in life, the answer-man.

I think it is Bhatkoo, said Iqbal.

So what? I said. Bhatkoo is the one who grabbed us and threw us from that place.

I think he is saying to go to the door and he will let us back into the building, said Iqbal.

But why? I do not want to be pushed and pulled and grabbed again, I said.

Then don't say stupid things and don't laugh at the plants, said Iqbal. He looked angry. Sometimes I feel you might be a silly bugger, he said.

I became worried. Iqbal does not say such things. He must be very angry.

Sorry, I said.

No problem, said Iqbal. I am sorry for implying that you might be a stupid bugger.

Silly, I said.

What? said Iqbal.

The implication was for silly bugger, I said. Implying that I am a stupid bugger is a totally different matter.

Okay, yes, I see, said Iqbal.

With all this silliness, we had forgotten about Bhatkoo

and the torch. We were reminded when Bhatkoo used the torch to make noises on the window glass.

Fine, I said, this matter is about truth, not silliness, so let us re-enter the dark building.

Fine, said Iqbal. You go first.

Why me? I said.

Because you got us removed from there, so it is your duty.

This seemed logical, and although I wanted to argue, I felt that time was of absolute value here. So I stood up straight and went to the door of the building and pushed it. The door was locked and pushing did not accomplish anything. I looked at Iqbal. He indicated that I should wait.

I waited, and presently the door made a clicking sound and opened and I entered the dim room. Iqbal followed me, and the door closed behind him. We stood in the semi-darkness and looked around. Bhatkoo was behind us, and he turned on the torch.

Okay now, said Bhatkoo, I will take you back inside, but you must be courteous towards the plants.

Okay, I said, but tell me one thing.

What is it, said Bhatkoo.

Why the politeness is necessary to plants? You all are madmen or what? I asked.

Then I heard a clucking sound from Iqbal, and I realized that asking people if they are madmen is something that falls within the category of impolite. Luckily Bhatkoo was not offended.

See, said Bhatkoo, Netaji spent many years in hiding with no company except for the plants. As a result, he is very friendly with plants and trees and such creatures. So please show some respect for this.

Okay, I said, will do.

I did not say much more, but in my mind I said many things. One thing was that Netaji must definitely be a madman even if he really is Netaji. After all, only madmen become so friendly with vegetative creatures. Of course, I did not voice such opinions.

We followed Bhatkoo down into the interiors of the building where it became darker and darker. Then we stopped at a large metallic door, at which point Bhatkoo switched off the torch.

What are you doing, I shouted.

Quiet, said Bhatkoo.

Yes, quiet, said Iqbal. Remember what I told you.

Okay, I said. And I became quiet. But internally I was worried.

The metallic door opened with a metallic sound and from inside came a bright white light almost as bright as the sun himself. I shouted in pain, but then quickly shut up from fear of impoliteness.

We entered through the door, and I opened my eyes to see a large room, so large that I could not see any walls. The lights hanging down from the ceiling were so bright that I could not see any ceiling. I averted my eyes in the downward direction, afraid that I would not be able to see any floor either, but thankfully the floor was clearly visible, and so I stepped onto it.

You impolite buggers are back I see, came a voice. It was the voice of Netaji.

I looked up and saw Netaji standing in my presence. He was smiling, and did not look angry anymore. I was thankful of this. I did not want to be subjected to more grabbing.

Hello Netaji, said Iqbal.

Yes, hello. Welcome to my hydroponic farm, he said. Then he gestured with his hand in a sweeping manner like someone displaying something to someone else, which was actually quite appropriate for the situation.

The room was indeed quite a sight. Hundreds, maybe thousands, of tables with glass tops and glass bottoms, each table holding different-different plants. The roots of the plants were plainly visible, all twisted and curly, but clean and without dirt. And the reason for lack of dirt seemed to be lack of soil. In fact the glass tables were glass tanks, and the glass tops were some kind of special holders that held the plants upright in the glass tanks. Of course, the lights were bright, even brighter than when the sun tries to shine through the Mumbai smog.

Oh my god, I said, what wondrousness.

I looked at Iqbal. He too was struck by wonder.

Netaji smiled, and Bhatkoo clapped.

Yes, I said, these are truly wondrous plants.

Louder, said Netaji.

What? I said.

Say it louder, he said.

What, I shouted.

Netaji held his own head and looked down. When he looked up he was laughing. You are a silly funny bugger, he said.

I smiled politely. Okay then, I said.

Netaji shook his head. Plants do not have ears, he said, but if you say something loudly, they can feel the vibrations, and if it is a polite thing, they get happy.

I smiled politely again. I did not say anything. This vibrations nonsense was even more proof that we were dealing with madmen. But still, there was no denying the wondrousness of the hydroponic garden. It was a beautiful garden, like something created by the gods themselves. It even smelled beautiful, although I could not see many flowers of fragrance.

Beautiful, I said. Then I spoke very loudly: Beautiful!

Netaji smiled at me. Good, he said.

Can we see the onion hydroponic? I asked.

Netaji smiled and shook his head. No, not now, he said. That is in a special section that is under lock and key. For political reasons, you see.

I did not see. But out of politeness I felt I should not ask. I looked to Iqbal, who nodded for me to go ahead and ask. So I proceeded.

Why is onion under political confinement? I asked.

Netaji's smile disappeared. It is a serious matter, he said, not something that can be easily explained to a funny bugger like yourself.

This seemed logical, even though I do not think of myself as a funny bugger.

Then Iqbal, my brother in life, came to the rescue.

Explain to me then, he said, because I am not a funny bugger whatsoever.

Netaji was quiet at first but then he spoke. Okay, he said, I will try. I will try and explain to you the political reasons behind the confinement of my hydroponic onions.

12

Come, said Netaji, let us go to the sitting area and have seats.

Okay, I said.

We followed Netaji as he led us in and out and between the rows and columns of glass-topped-and-bottomed tables and tanks. Presently we arrived at a wall, and in that wall was a doorway which had no door. I mean there was a cutout in the wall in the shape of a door, but no actual door was affixed.

The sitting area contained ample seating for the three of us. I say three because this Bhatkoo chap had disappeared again without any notice and without us noticing. Very strange, but I did not worry. At least there was no darkness in this place. Quite the opposite in fact—too much light for a simple seating area. But I did not complain for fear of angering the plants and by default Netaji himself.

So, said Netaji. He looked at Iqbal and nodded.

Iqbal nodded in reply.

You want to know the reason why my onion garden is under lock and key, is it? Netaji asked.

Yes, said Iqbal.

First tell me this, said Netaji.

What? said Iqbal.

I see you have beard, said Netaji.

Iqbal looked at me and then looked at Netaji. Yes, he said, I have beard.

Are you Muslim? said Netaji.

Yes indeed, said Iqbal.

I see, said Netaji.

I was curious as to these questions. Netaji was not showing any expression on face or in voice, and I could not tell if these were polite questions or serious questions. Not that politeness is not serious, but you know my meaning. Iqbal of course was as expressionless as Netaji during this polite interrogation.

Netaji continued with the questioning. You have relatives in Pakistan? he asked.

No, said Iqbal, I am hundred percent seventh generation Mumbaikar.

Don't worry, said Netaji, it is only a polite question. Don't be afraid to say so if you have relatives in Pakistan.

I would not be afraid, said Iqbal, but I have no such thing to say.

Okay, said Netaji, then I will continue with my explanation.

Excellent, said Iqbal.

I leaned forward so I could hear better. Netaji gave me a look from the side of his eyes, but he did not say anything to me. Still, out of politeness, I moved back little bit.

See, said Netaji, our historical border situation in the northern provinces has been quite touchy for the last sixty or seventy years.

Yes, said Iqbal, if you mean our borders with Pakistan and China and not so much our borders with Nepal and Bhutan.

Yes, yes, that is what I mean, said Netaji, the big problematic borders.

Now Netaji went quiet for many minutes, and I wondered if he had fallen asleep with his eyes open and sitting upright. But no, he presently came back to the present and continued.

You are Gandhians, yes? he asked.

Yes, said Iqbal.

Yes, I said.

You know that MK and myself were closely acquainted in the old days, yes? said Netaji.

MK? I asked.

Mohandas Karamchand Gandhi, said Netaji, but I called him MK, and he did not mind it.

Okay, yes, said Iqbal. He gave me a look that meant be careful, this could be an explosive situation. I did not know at that time why Iqbal gave me that look. But soon I realized it was because historical records suggest that Gandhiji and Netaji had several major disagreements during the independence movement.

You know, said Netaji, history books will say that I had disagreements with MK.

Iqbal nodded but did not say anything. I did not even nod.

This was true in the early days, said Netaji, but the differences were dissolved by around 1942-43, even though this is not what the history books will say.

Iqbal nodded again.

Of course, I was not welcome in India around that time, partly because of my supposed opposition to MK and alleged connection to the Nazi party, said Netaji. He went quiet and he looked sad. That connection, he said, was exaggerated, although during the days of my disagreements with MK I may have believed that India needed a strong and merciless autocrat like that bloody bastard Adolf.

Iqbal nodded.

But it was not because I shared any of that bastard's views or beliefs, said Netaji.

No, said Iqbal, you were known to be a champion of the equality of all people.

Yes, said Netaji, I am happy to hear it.

And I am happy to say it, said Iqbal.

Happy, I shouted.

Netaji gave me a look that possibly meant I should shut up. I did not want to take any risks, so I shut up.

Anyway, said Netaji, I was a young man then, full of need for immediate action and quick results, no matter what the cost. It was said that I said I would shake hands with the devil himself if it meant freedom for India.

Iqbal stared at Netaji and nodded slowly. I quietly put my hands behind my back.

Of course, I did not actually say that, said Netaji, but it is something I would have said and in fact maybe I said it—who knows—it was seventy or eighty years ago now.

Iqbal nodded. Yes, he said, sometimes memory fails little bit after seventy-plus years.

But regardless, said Netaji, the benefits of my exile from India is the full crux of my point.

What benefits? asked Iqbal.

See, said Netaji, during my exile I travelled around the East Asia region, during which point my supposed death occurred in a plane crash over Taiwan.

Yes, said Iqbal, that is indeed the historical record of your death, although there have been some that said you were alive and well.

Yes, said Netaji, I was quite alive, and after the war I spent some time in Japan.

Okay, said Iqbal.

Yes, said Netaji, wonderful land and people, fish-lovers like myself, but not so much double-fried fish.

No, said Iqbal, they like the raw fish.

Yes yes, said Netaji, but that is not the crux of the point.

Okay sorry, said Iqbal, please go on to the crux.

The crux, said Netaji, is that Japan is small in land mass but large in people number.

Okay, said Iqbal.

I looked at Iqbal, and I could see that his mental wheels were turning, and so I said nothing.

And due to this discrepancy, said Netaji, they are motivated to arrive at many inventions and discoveries.

Okay, said Iqbal. He smiled, and I could see that Iqbal had arrived at a conclusion.

Yes, said Netaji, I see you are following me.

Indeed, said Iqbal.

So what you see here, said Netaji, is the wondrous fusion of invention and discovery that is a direct result of my exile that took me to Japan.

Netaji pointed in the direction of the large hydroponic garden that lay behind the wall that enclosed the seating area.

Iqbal smiled again. Yes, he said, I see.

I for one did not see the crux of the point or even the point itself. How this all related to the political confinement situation of the onion hydroponic I did not know. Since I had been reduced to a silly funny bugger who was not encouraged to speak, I simply sat quietly in my seat and sulked. Right now I was thinking more about the onion bhajias than of any political confinement issues. I almost asked for the bhajias, but then held my tongue out of politeness.

Would you like some onion bhajias? said Netaji. He looked at me and then at Iqbal.

No no, said Iqbal, you must continue with the crux of the point at hand.

I almost stood up and slapped Iqbal for his selfishness and lack of compassion. After all, he should have known that I was thinking about those bhajias. Iqbal is my brother in life. He knows my thought patterns, and in this case he must have willingly ignored my thought patterns and substituted his own thought patterns to take advantage of the situation. But the question had been asked to the both of us, so I decided to speak up for myself.

Yes, I said, I would like onion bhajias.

Iqbal held his head and shook it back and forth. I knew

what he was thinking, but I did not care. Netaji made an offer, and I accepted the offer. It was quite simple, and I saw no harm in it.

Excellent, said Netaji.

He stood up and went close to the door-shaped cutout in the wall leading to the large hydroponic garden. He made some sounds in Bengali, and immediately Bhatkoo and two or three other people showed up in the door-shaped cutout area. Netaji said some things to them, then he pointed at me, and then all of them laughed. I smiled at them. I did not care if they thought of me as a funny bugger, at least not as long as I got some onion bhajias.

13

The onion bhajias came quickly and went quickly also. I polished off ninety-two percent of the seventeen onion bhajias placed before me. Iqbal did not notice because he was used to such things, and Netaji did not seem to mind. I saw that Bhatkoo and those other chaps were watching me from the door-shaped cutout, but I did not care about them.

Now, said Netaji, we can continue with the crux at hand.

May I have some water? I asked.

Iqbal looked slightly angry, but not so much. After all, to deny a thirsty man water is to commit an act of violence against him, and we were Gandhians, men of nonviolence.

Presently the water came, and I consumed it with appropriate quickness and respect. Bhatkoo took the empty glass from me and yet again disappeared into some unseen space in the brightly lit room.

Now, said Netaji, we can continue.

Yes, said Iqbal.

I meant to speak, but only some gas emerged from my mouth.

Iqbal quickly continued. So Netaji, he said, the hydroponics technology has been appropriated from the Japanese, is it?

Netaji nodded. Yes and no. Some of the knowledge comes from there, but the electronics and lights and seeds and water and nutrient concentrates are of course Indian.

I nodded wisely and with a smile to show my Indian pride.

But now it seemed Iqbal was the one with the incisive and borderline dangerous questions.

But Netaji, said Iqbal, if the ingredients and infrastructure is all Indian, then what is the political sensitivity of the hydroponics? Why is it not being used for the benefit of onion problems? Why? And why not?

Netaji looked down at the highly reflective tiled floor, but I could tell he was not angry. He may even have been smiling, although it could also have been an expression of eye pain due to excessive light from said reflectiveness.

Now he looked up and smiled. Some problems are bigger than onion problem, he said.

I was about to protest loudly and with anger, but yet again simply gas escaped from my open mouth, and so I remained in my thoughtful and quiet position of agreement. I looked at Iqbal, who was surprisingly calm. I say surprising because the onion problem must have been weighing heavily on his thin head.

But Iqbal simply nodded wisely. And by wisely I mean not like how I previously nodded to make others think I was wise. No, Iqbal must be really understanding what this madman is saying.

Border disputes, said Iqbal.

Netaji smiled, and now he nodded wisely.

I almost shouted with anger. After all, we have already established that all border disputes are directly related to the onion problem. Still, out of fear of releasing more gas, and possibly appearing unwise, I kept quiet and let these other two wise men talk.

Yes, said Netaji, causes of border disputes are many of course, and it is not up to one or two of us to ascertain and address such matters of immense gravity.

I nodded again.

But, said Netaji, we can do something to help. And that is what I am doing.

Now Iqbal was still, and he began to touch his beard, which meant he was thinking of a question.

Netaji appeared to anticipate a question, and he interjected with his own question. Smart bugger, this madman.

Tell me, said Netaji, why is it we have not had wars with Pakistan and China for over ten years now?

We were both quiet.

Netaji smiled. He appeared to be very satisfied by his unanswerable question. Unanswerable by us only, it seems, because Netaji himself proceeded to answer it.

Onions, he said.

Onions? I asked.

Netaji smiled again. See, he said, India is a big exporter of onions to many countries. Countries that include Pakistan and China.

But how and why? I said. After all, China occupies number one rank in onion production. How can we send our nice round onions to them when there is onion problem here itself?

That is the thing, said Netaji, when there is onion problem here, we do not send our nice round onions to our neighbors in the north.

Okay, I said, that is sensible.

No, said Netaji.

What? I said.

Yes, said Netaji. See, onion problems in Pakistan and China are as big as problems here in India. Bigger even, since there are no Jains in those countries, and therefore a much higher percentage of the population consumes onions.

I nodded. Yes, these Jains have caused many onion problems.

Netaji laughed and shook his head. You are a silly bugger, he said. No, really, quite silly. Jains are not causing any problems anywhere. Please leave them out of this, you silly bugger.

Iqbal also looked at me as if I was the madman and not this other madman who says he is Netaji. But regardless, due to being outnumbered, I looked down as if to say sorry.

Sorry, said Iqbal, he is a silly bugger, but he means well.

Yes, I see, said Netaji.

Sorry, I said.

No matter, said Netaji, let us continue.

Okay, said Iqbal.

As I was saying, said Netaji, onion problems in Pakistan and China cause lots of social upheaval, and hence the government starts to feel pressure. And this pressure can be rebounded to India in the form of border attacks and other such nonsense that distracts the people from the onion problems. See, onion shortage becomes less of a problem if you can immediately create other bigger problems such as war.

So you are saying that decrease in onion exports from India to Pakistan and China can lead to war sometimes? asked Iqbal.

Not sometimes, said Netaji, all the time. All the previous wars were directly related to drop in Indian onion exports. If you study the correlations of failure of Indian onion crop with increase in border disputes, you will find a hundred percent correlation.

But correlation does not imply causation, I said with my one finger raised in the air for dramatic effect.

Netaji and Iqbal stared at me as if I had turned into a Bombay-duck.

Sorry, I said.

They did not say anything. I think they were shocked at my precise and timely comment. As I mentioned before, maths is my strong suit.

Netaji now looked at me and smiled and nodded. Yes, my silly friend. You are quite correct. But what if I told you that exactly one year prior to each border dispute, the onion crop had failed, leading to cancellation of onion exports?

That would still not guarantee causation, I said with confidence and perhaps some obstinence.

No, said Netaji, no guarantee, but there is strong indication, would you not agree?

Yes, I said.

Yes, said Iqbal.

Okay, so to continue to the crux of my point, said Netaji, every time India stops sending onions to Pakistan and China, they reply by sending missiles and soldiers.

That is not fair, I said.

Very rude, said Iqbal.

Netaji laughed. Yes, he said, unfair and rude, but not unexpected given the lack of good democratic government in Pakistan and China.

I do not follow, I said.

Iqbal was quiet. I could see he was thinking, but I could also see that he did not follow Netaji's reasoning.

See, said Netaji, in these non-democratic countries, the rulers are in constant fear of revolution. And since it is very easy for these rulers to make rules, they can start border disputes with just one or two simple rulings.

I was still confused, but Iqbal was smiling.

Okay, said Iqbal, and since onion problem is the number one reason for revolution, when there is onion problem in non-democratic countries, the rulers create border disputes to distract the people. That is what you are trying to explain to us.

Yes, said Netaji.

Iqbal and I were quiet once again. The conversation was very complicated, and I was not sure if it was over or not. I thought about my wife, and I became hungry again.

So, said Netaji.

So, said Iqbal.

Okay, I said, shall we take leave then?

You Gandhians have had enough truth for one day? said Netaji.

Iqbal looked at me.

I made a sound.

Iqbal was still looking at me when I stopped making sounds.

No, I said, there can never be enough truth.

Netaji laughed. Good, he said, because you have not yet found out why my hydroponic onions are under lock and key.

It is obvious now, I said.

Okay, said Netaji, then explain it.

See, I said, when there is onion problem in India, you release your hydroponic onions to the Indian market to offset the problem. And so you must keep the onions locked up so that you can control the delivery and timing of said delivery. Simple.

Yes, said Iqbal, simple and patriotic.

Very much so, I said.

Netaji is indeed a great freedom fighter, said Iqbal.

Thank you, thank you, said Netaji, but you are all wrong about everything except the fact of my patriotism.

Again we were quiet.

Netaji leaned back in his chair and looked around the brightly lit room as if to make sure no one was hiding. See, he said, I actually supply my hydroponic onions directly to Pakistani and Chinese groups.

We were still quiet, but in stunned state.

After some time I spoke.

But Netaji, I said.

Netaji shook his head. See, he said, my hydroponics do not produce sufficient output to affect Indian national supply enough to maintain exports during local onion crisis.

Okay, I said.

So, said Netaji, I am left with two choices—one is to supply only the Bombay region with onions, and the other is to supply only certain groups in Pakistan and China with onions.

What groups, asked Iqbal.

In Pakistan it is mainly the big groups like Taliban and Lakshar-e-Taibba, said Netaji, and in China it is the Maoist rebel groups.

It is hard now to describe our feelings of confusion. The bright lights were creating havoc with my sense of balance and sanity, and if I was not so round, I would surely have gotten up to run away from this madman.

Do not be afraid, said Netaji, it is not what it seems.

Then what is it? said Iqbal.

Netaji laughed. Did I not say I was a patriot?

Actually I said it, I said.

No, I said it, said Iqbal.

Does not matter who said it, said Netaji.

Okay, I said.

Iqbal was quiet, and I could tell he was thinking of a way to escape from this madman, but was conflicted by our pledge to pursue the truth. Although, to be honest, I did not think that such danger to our own lives should be necessary for pursuit of truth. At least not on the first day of pursuing truth. Again I thought of my wife, and I felt sad that since this madman was undoubtedly going to murder us, I would not see her again. My dear, sweet wife. So much love for her I felt in that moment under the bright lights.

Then I felt hungry again, and so I paid attention to the madman.

He was still laughing, but not so much like a madman. More like someone who was playing a trick on us.

See, said Netaji, I will give you an example of the problem and my solution.

Okay, I said.

Yes, said Iqbal.

Now imagine there is an onion problem and exports to Pakistan have been cut, said Netaji.

Okay, said Iqbal.

Wait one minute, I said.

They both looked at me.

Okay, I said, I am ready.

Now, said Netaji, low exports means onion problem in Pakistan, which increases chances for revolution because people are getting angry because their food does not taste so good without onions.

Yes, I said, that Pakistani food is very much dependent on onions.

Okay, said Netaji, so the rulers get some of these angry groups like Taliban and Lakshar to recruit some angry Pakistani villagers to launch attacks along the border with India and Kashmir, and then all the local Pakistanis become occupied with all that militant nonsense.

Ah, said Iqbal, and so the locals are not so worried about their food being less tasty.

Ah, I said, and so they are less interested in starting internal revolutions. It is simple misdirection of aggression.

Yes, said Netaji, yes.

And so logically, said Iqbal, if you supply onions directly to angry groups like Taliban and Lakshar, perhaps they will become less angry, and maybe they will be less motivated to recruit angry villagers to launch attacks.

Yes, said Netaji, and hence I am a patriot.

I thought about this for some time. It seemed logical, but still something was off.

But Netaji, I said, by depriving Indian locals of your onions, are you not creating angry conditions in the homeland?

Iqbal looked at me and nodded.

And so, I said, are you not increasing chances for revolution here as well?

Iqbal nodded again.

Now with Iqbal's support, I gained confidence in my logic. So, I said, would our rulers also not start to launch border nonsense to create distractions for the angry people who have no onions? Would our rulers also not be afraid of revolution?

Netaji laughed. No, he said, we have a democracy in India. Here when there is revolution, some politicians temporarily give up their jobs to their cousins and in-laws, and then when the onion problem is solved, they simply regain their jobs.

It is a good system, I said.

Iqbal shook his head and looked at the tiles.

Then Netaji became serious. But, he said, you are little bit correct in your earlier point. Nowadays, the politicians are finding that after giving up their jobs to cousins and in-laws, there is no guarantee that they will regain their jobs. And so they are more concerned with onion problem than previously.

Okay, I said, so now you will be changing your onion supply plan?

No, you silly bugger, said Netaji, I do not care about the family matters of the stupid politicians.

But to return to an even earlier point, said Iqbal, if the Indian politicians are worrying about onion problem and revolution, then would they not create border trouble to distract the Indians?

Netaji laughed. No, he said, the Indian politicians simply create internal trouble to distract the people.

Like what? I said.

Like riots, floods, earthquakes, temple destruction, mosque burning, and other such normal day-to-day things, said Netaji.

Now again Iqbal and I were stunned.

But, I said, is that not worse for Indians than border trouble?

Yes, said Iqbal, should you not then redirect your onions to local people so that such terrible domestic problems can be reduced?

Netaji sighed and shook his head.

What is the problem? I asked.

See, said Netaji, although you will soon understand that my tactics provide the maximum possible benefit to India's overall situation, the problems you speak of are domestic issues, and I am a foreign-relations specialist, so these are not my problems to deal with directly.

Now I was hundred percent sure we were dealing with a madman. Or perhaps even a politician himself, which could be even more dangerous. I looked at Iqbal, and I could tell by his stillness that he agreed with me. We somehow had to stop this madman, or at least get ourselves out of there.

14

Of course, when you are in the darkness of a madman's hole in a previously-unknown courtyard in the city of your birth, then sometimes it is not so easy to get out, or even to talk about getting out. You see, for some reason Iqbal was not paying as much attention to me, and I worried that our wavelengths were little bit off at that point, the result being that I was unable to communicate my determination to get away from the madman. At least I could not communicate it through nonverbal and nonphysical means.

So first I selected a physical means of communication. With my foot, I poked Iqbal's foot. But this did not work. He simply moved his foot to the side and kept on staring at Netaji. So then I tried a verbal means of communicating my apprehension.

Since Netaji was highly trained in diplomacy, I had to be diplomatic, so I could not simply say: Come Iqbal, let us flee from this dark hole of the madman who thinks he is Netaji.

Instead, I made sounds that I hoped would be understood by Iqbal and not Netaji. The sounds themselves are indescribable, and even if they were describable, it would not do to describe them. Suffice it to say that I started off with the softest and least offensive sounds, and progressively progressed to the loudest and most disgusting sounds.

Perhaps you have eaten too many onion bhajias, said Netaji with a diplomatic smile.

Iqbal stared at me as if to say the same thing but with the addition of shut up at the end. I was quite embarrassed, and when I looked up to see Bhatkoo peeking at me through the door-shaped opening in the wall, I became angry like how when you are embarrassed and someone laughs at you and you immediately become angry. But luckily the anger was of the clarifying kind, and I immediately thought of a solution to being expelled from this dark hole of the madmen and the hydroponics.

I would insult the plants once more. No doubt then Iqbal and I would be thrown from the place with a high degree of immediacy and prejudice. Although I thought the idea of plants that care about what we have to say was quite silly, I knew that sometimes you have to pursue silly ideas when dealing with madmen.

Of course, there were no plants in the brightly lit sitting room where we were sitting, so I stood up from my seat and asked for a toilet.

You will have to go to the toilet, said Netaji, because the toilet cannot be brought to you.

Yes yes of course, I said while ignoring Iqbal's look of embarrassment. It did not matter what my brother in life thought of me at this point. When I succeeded in getting us ejected and expunged from this place, he would understand and we would be like brothers once again.

So Bhatkoo entered, and with the dirty smirk of a servant of a powerful madman, he led me out of the sitting room.

Clearing space for the Bombay-duck? said Bhatkoo with a smirk.

Bombay-duck? I said in panic.

Yes, said Bhatkoo, the Netaji has ordered some to be prepared for your friend and you. Double-fried with extra-double salt.

Now I was worried. I knew that Iqbal was a small eater even at the biggest of occasions, but when it came to Bombay-duck, there was no equal on the western coasts of India. Part of this I think came from the fact that Iqbal's wife did all the cooking in the house, and although she is a sweet thing and is very nice to Iqbal, she refuses to cook Bombay-duck on account of the smell. And so, when you are denied something at home on a regular basis, then when you are offered that thing outside on an irregular basis, you tend to overdo it. And this was the case with Iqbal and the Bombay-duck.

I thought some more on the topic as I expunged myself in the toilet. At first my confidence and resolve wavered, but soon it passed and I felt light and refreshed and ready to insult those bloody plants. Sometimes a man must upset his brother in order to save the man who is blinded by the spicy charms of the slender and salty Bombay-duck. In this case my brother was also the man blinded by said spicy charms, and so I stepped out into the hydroponic garden and looked around for a suitable candidate to abuse.

Close to me there were some tomato hydroponics. Now I remembered that after speaking with the pao-bhaji-walla I had decided that tomatoes were less perfect and hence less desirable than onions, and so I thought this was a sign for me to abuse these tomato plants. Of course, personally I love the tomato, but I could not imagine that this sweet red bulbous plant would lose much sleep over my abuse. After all, if the plant was smart enough to understand that I am abusing it, then it should be wise enough to note that I am under the pressure of being in the dark bulbous hole of a madman, and I am only trying to save myself and my brother in life.

So I confidently and lightly stepped forward and stood next to the red sweet tomato and took a deep breath, looking around to make sure that Bhatkoo and a few other attendants were close enough to hear my abuses.

You stupid red bulbous blob of redness, I said.

I waited for a reaction from either the plant or the attendants, but neither party seemed to notice. So I stepped closer and spoke louder.

Ay, you bloody tomato with your funny face and ugly smell, I said.

Now Bhatkoo looked over at me with suspicion, but still he did not approach. Instead, he gestured to some other attendants, three of whom came to Bhatkoo to see what he was gesturing about. Now I had an audience, and so I pulled out the big ones.

Perhaps if you were an onion you would get more respect, I said to the innocent-looking tomato, but you are just a silly tomato and deserving of not even a private room with lock-and-key.

At this point I swore the tomato fruits moved a little bit. At first I thought it was the wind, but we were in a dark hole with no fans and so no wind. Obviously it was my imagination. Or perhaps I was weak and fragile and hallucinating due to not having eaten lunch yet. After all, since morning I had only consumed toast, jam, butter, tea, milk, sugar, pao-bhaji, and onion bhajias. That is not enough to sustain a man in such times of national, international, and personal crisis. Then suddenly I got the sweet charming smell of Bombay-duck frying to perfection in spices and salt and sunflower oil. Even though I am not a big fan of Bombay-duck, in times of emergency, one must make do with what is served.

But then I gathered myself once again and re-firmed my resolve. I told myself I would not fall victim to the charms of the slender Bombay-duck. I am a Gandhian, and the Gandhian must hold firm to his vows when times are tough. After all, did Bapuji not refuse milk even when he was near death due to dehydration and dysentery? Did the great Mahatma not refute temptation even when being washed by the women who served him?

I thought of my wife and then immediately thought of food and my resolve wavered yet again and my legs trembled and I almost reached out for one of the succulent sweet-sweet tomatoes that beckoned to me like bulbous balls of temptation and sweetness.

You dirty thing, I screamed at the tomato, how dare you look at me that way. I am a married man, you know.

Now Bhatkoo and the attendants had moved closer to me, and this gave me some confidence and a boost of energy needed to push my self-sacrificing act to completion. So I pushed on.

Your redness is offensive and disgusting, I said with disdain, and your bulbousness is dirty and corrosive to the soul.

I paused and looked over at Bhatkoo and the others. And only at this point did I notice that they were neither angry nor upset but instead were amused at my attempts at abuse. This made me angrier, and I started to yell at the tomato plants and spoke great obscenities in many different Indian languages. The obscenities I cannot repeat here, partly because they would not be understood in the translation, and if they were understood, this account would immediately be classified as pornographic material and seized by the government and burned with great immediacy and precision.

So suffice it to say that the obscenities I hurled were of graphic and terrible nature, and the volume and intensity at which I hurled them were of admirable depth. But still neither Bhatkoo nor the attendants, all of whom had no doubt heard my abusive advances, made any move to have me thrown out of the deep dark place of the madman and his soil-less plant life.

And so I decided I would launch a physical assault on the tomato.

15

As I prepared myself to attack the innocent sweet tomato, I wondered if perhaps I was committing a transgression towards the Gandhian principle of nonviolence. After all, a tomato is a form of life, is it not? And even though the idea that it can hear abusive language is laughable (as I have proven through my merciless abuses that registered no effect), a physical assault is abuse of a different class and nature. I tried to think back over Gandhiji's autobiography to see if he had allowed for violence under some exceptional situations, but my memory is not so good, and if there was such a passage in his book, I could not recall it.

But that is just as well, because my hesitation at that point was enough to obtain some success towards the ultimate goal of expungement and ejection of me and my brother in life.

As I stood there in my attack-stance, thinking about the life story of Gandhiji, one of the sweet innocent tomatoes began to gently sway. Presently, to my shock and awe, the tomato detached itself from its green moist dirt-less vine. I worried that perhaps the tomato will come after me, but of course it is a small fruit with no legs and so it just fell down straight into the glass container with a gentle sound not unlike that of a soft round object falling on hard flat glass.

I was frozen, unsure if my abuses had caused this detachment. I carefully looked over at the attendants, but miraculously they seemed to have lost interest in my interactions with the tomato hydroponic, and in fact Bhatkoo was not even standing there anymore. And so I found myself alone with my felled victim, the innocent tomato, the red bulb of sweetness that did not deserve my abuses but received them nonetheless. I had committed an act of violence, and though the act itself had been successful, my ultimate goal had been left unfulfilled. What a terrible position for a Gandhian to be in, and I felt appropriately terrible. I stepped up to the fallen ball of redness and reached out to caress its fallen form, but a loud voice stopped me and I remained there frozen, arm outstretched, my crime apparent for all to see and laugh at.

Bombay-ducks are here, shouted Bhatkoo from across the hydroponic garden.

I swallowed hard. Could it be that no one had witnessed my hate-crime? Could it be that all of it was a hallucination due to lack of food and excessive lightness in the stomach and therefore head? Better not to take any chances, I thought, and so I pocketed the tomato and hurried to the door-shaped opening where the slender Bombay-duck sang her song of victory.

After sitting down in the sitting area, I stayed quiet and did not speak even when spoken to. Iqbal was looking at me in a way I had not seen him look before, and Netaji was looking at Iqbal in a way that I could not interpret. Finally Netaji turned to me and smiled.

You may keep that tomato, he said.

I was speechless, and quickly checked my pocket to see if the tomato was visible. It was not. I looked up and my eyes locked with the dark dancing eyes of Bhatkoo, the madman's servant. His eyes told me he had observed all and reported all, and my respect for this Bhatkoo increased from the previous level of low to the current level of medium. Crafty bugger, this Bhatkoo. And observant as well.

Now Netaji turned back to Iqbal. And your onions will be packaged and brought out to you shortly, he said.

Thank you, said Iqbal.

I stared at Iqbal in wonder and delight. Onions. This meant that Iqbal's onion problem had been solved. Our pursuit had reached the end, and although the truth was still not so clear to me, the fact that our initial problem had been solved meant that the truth had been pursued to some degree of success. Perhaps later reflection would reveal the truth in its simplest and most beautiful form, but for now we could celebrate our successful completion of the first serious Gandhian pursuit launched by myself and Iqbal, my Gandhian brother in life.

At this point Netaji rose up and stepped away from the seating area to speak with Bhatkoo, and I took advantage of this moment of semi-privacy to congratulate my brother on solving his onion problem.

So now we can go, I said to him with relief.

No, he said quietly.

Ah okay, I replied, you want to eat the Bombay-duck first.

Yes, he said quietly.

No problem, I said, even I will eat the slender charming Duck with you in celebration.

Iqbal simply nodded.

And then we can go, I said to him with relief and some relish as the smell of spicy fried fish invaded my senses.

No, said Iqbal.

Means what, I said.

Means now we are part of this group, said Iqbal, and so this is our place now.

Means what, I said.

Means we are new recruits to Netaji's Hydroponic Foreign Policy Institute, he said, and this means we have duties to perform before our activation is complete and we are allowed outside this building and courtyard on our own.

Means what, I said again. But now my tone had changed from relief and confusion to panic and convolution.

Means we cannot go home until some tasks are performed to Netaji's satisfaction, said Iqbal.

What bloody tasks, I asked. I knew there could be no satisfying a madman, and so I wondered if I would ever see my wife again.

Mind your language please, said Netaji. He had returned behind my back, and now he stood in front of my front.

Sorry, I said, but Iqbal was just updating me on this unacceptable situation of not being allowed to leave this place.

Yes, said Netaji, you are both new recruits, and there has to be some breaking-in period before you can be trusted with the secrets that have been revealed to you.

What secrets, I shouted. You have not even told us how to avoid worry like you promised.

True, said Netaji with a smile and a laugh.

So tell us, I shouted again.

Sorry, said Netaji, the promise of the secret of worry-avoidance is just a recruiting tactic to bring in the people who are gullible and simple but yet idealistic enough to believe that a world without worry is possible or even desirable.

So you lied to us, I said in Gandhian fury.

Netaji shrugged his shoulders. I told you two truths and one lie, he said, and so I am majority truthful, and what more can you ask of a foreign policy expert?

This seemed logical enough and so I calmed down and Netaji continued.

No, he said, the real secret is this place and these people.

What people, I shouted.

Myself, said Netaji.

I stared at the madman and then at Iqbal, who was simply looking at his onions and rubbing them like rubbing them would free us from this predicament.

See, said Netaji, it would not do for people to find out that I am still alive and well.

Why not? I said. Will people not be overjoyed? Will they not celebrate your life and bring you to the forefront of India's foreign policy once more?

Netaji smiled. My bulbous friend, he said, I am already at the forefront of India's foreign policy. And soon the both of you will be there with me as well.

You are a madman, I said, and we are leaving this dark hole of yours.

I stood up and looked at Iqbal for support. But my brother in life did not meet my eye, and he simply clutched his packet of onions and stared into the distance as if there was something of interest far away. There was not, and this meant that Iqbal was avoiding looking at me. I was alone once more, with nothing but my one tomato to stand with me. So I pulled out the tomato and held it up for all to see.

I will squash this, I said to Netaji.

Netaji smiled. Now who is the madman, he said.

You are the madman, I said, and I will squash this tomato and all the other hydroponics will know that you will not defend them when they are in danger of being squashed.

You do not know very much about these plants, said Netaji with a smile.

I know enough, I said.

No, said Netaji, because then you would know that the survival of the tomato species depends on stupid animals like you taking the red sweet fruit of the plant and squashing it and spreading its seeds. The threat of squashing it is not a threat at all, and in fact the tomato plants and all other hydroponics will marvel at my ability to get stupid animals like you to spread their seeds.

Now I felt like a silly bugger again. I had abused the tomato fruit, not the mother plant. The tomato fruit must have been fine with the abuses because an animal that abuses the fruit is perhaps more likely to squash the fruit and hence spread the seeds. This must be why Bhatkoo and the attendants made no move to stop my abuses. My spirit shattered, my resolve reduced, my determination destroyed, I dropped the triumphant tomato and sat down and filled up my plate with seven or eight Bombay-ducks.

16

RK-sahib, said Netaji after the Bombay-ducks were consumed, perhaps things have become a little too combative and tense between us all.

I was full, but not full enough to forget our situation. Perhaps, I said.

See, said Netaji, I would not ask you to do anything that violates your Gandhian principles. At the end of it, one could say I am a Gandhian myself. And the task I have set for you and Iqbalji is one that would be near and dear to Bapuji's heart.

I had my doubts about what this madman would have us do, but since the Bombay-duck was much better than my expectation of it, it stood to reason that perhaps the task would be better than expectation as well.

What is it, I said as I licked a piece of salty spice from my fingers.

Iqbal knows the details, said Netaji, and so he will explain it to you.

Iqbal nodded as I stared at him in surprise.

When did you learn of all this, I asked Iqbal.

When you were outside in the toilet, said Iqbal.

Okay, I said non-combatively because I did not want to draw attention to my previous Himalayan miscalculation of abusing the tomato fruit and not the mother plant itself.

I will leave you two for a while to talk, said Netaji. He got up and left, but not without a very meaningful look at Iqbal and an even more meaningful pat on the shoulders of Iqbal, my brother in life, the brother who was making plans to do something for a madman just because the madman had provided him with some onions.

It is not just for the onions, said Iqbal as he clutched his packet of onions like a squirrel clutching a stolen samosa.

Okay fine, I said, whatever you say.

No, said Iqbal, do not talk like that.

Okay fine, I said again.

Netaji may be a little bit cracked, he said, but he is not dangerous.

Okay fine, I said, then let us do his cracked job and then take leave of this place forever.

Now Iqbal looked at me with that same long face that he had displayed with great success at the beginning of our Gandhian adventures when we had made the fateful decision even before the tea had cooled. The decision to pursue the truth wherever he or she may lie, and whatever gender the truth may be. So I took a big sigh and leaned back in my chair and made some hand signals that indicated that I understood Iqbal's look and that he should proceed with the explanation of our task.

Our task, said Iqbal, is for the continuity of Netaji's undercover relations with extremist groups in Pakistan.

I sat quietly and tried to digest that statement, but digestion is not easy when the blood is boiling.

Those bastards, I shouted, they have killed hundreds and hundreds of innocent Indians and other peoples.

Yes, said Iqbal, but they have actually killed thousands and thousands of Pakistanis as well.

Fine, I said while still shouting, so that makes those bastards even worse.

Oh yes, said Iqbal, they are very very bad people.

Then why must we have any relations with them, I shouted, other than the relation of justice coming down upon their dirty hairy faces with great immediacy and extreme prejudice.

Remember what Netaji told us, said Iqbal, sometimes you have to shake the hand of a devil to secure peace and freedom.

I thought he said that he did not actually say that but people just said that he said it, I said.

Yes maybe, said Iqbal, but that is not the actual crux.

Now you are sounding like the madman, I said, with your talk of devils and cruxes.

The crux, said Iqbal, is that Netaji's onion relationships with these bearded extremists generates peace in Pakistani villages and towns, and so people have less cause to kill each other or attack our border troops.

So our Mumbai people will have to go without onions while the Pakistani villagers eat biryani with extra-double-onion, I said.

Iqbal nodded and shrugged. Only for a short time, he said, until the Indian onion supply is increased through normal methods.

And at this point I was struck by a brainwave that showed me how the Indian onion supply could be increased through abnormal methods. We would divert the madman's hydroponic onions to the Mumbai market. Quite a simple plan, really. So I told it to Iqbal.

And so, I said in conclusion, the increase in Indian onion supply will bring domestic peace and good health, and will make the Indian people more resistant to terror attacks and border skirmishes.

That is a stupid plan, said Iqbal, and you are focusing only on domestic issues and ignoring the larger foreign relations issues that are at play here.

Ah, I said, suddenly you are an expert in foreign policy, is it?

Not suddenly, said Iqbal, I have been an expert for many years due to my deep ties to Pakistan and the Pakistani people.

I stared at Iqbal in surprise. Earlier he had denied any ties with Pakistan, and so my surprise was purely related to Iqbal's deliberate concealment of the truth. Other than that, ties with Pakistan is not such a problem. After all, the Indian and Pakistani people are one and the same, sisters like Hindi and Urdu, or brothers like myself and Iqbal. But now my brother had made two diametrically opposite statements today, and my boiling blood began to beckon me to seek the truth in this small matter before moving on to the larger matters of onion relationships with Pakistani terrorist groups.

Yes, said Iqbal, actually my entire mother's side of the family is from Pakistani Lahore.

Okay, I said, why did you not say so earlier then?

Because, said Iqbal, at that point I was not sure of Netaji's purpose in asking me such focused questions.

But that means you lied, I said, when you were committed to unwavering pursuit of the ways of Gandhi and the truth.

Commitment to the truth does not mean you cannot lie once in a while, said Iqbal, especially when it comes to foreign relations issues.

But neither me nor Netaji is foreign, I said.

You are not foreign, said Iqbal, but Netaji in fact is foreign.

What, I said with a laugh, how can that be?

Because, said Iqbal, since Netaji was considered dead and out of the country before 1947 when India gained independence, he never became a citizen of free India.

How can that be, I said, there are birthright rights and what-not.

Those rights and laws are not clear, said Iqbal, and so I did not want to volunteer sensitive foreign relations information at that point to someone who could be a non-citizen of India.

But so now you have clarified with Netaji through direct questioning? I asked.

Yes, said Iqbal, and he has confirmed that he is a citizen of no country at this point.

How can that be? I said.

How it can be I just explained, said Iqbal.

But he is a madman, I said, just another Indian madman.

Could a madman have remained without wrinkles for over

a hundred years? Could a madman have survived by wandering from Taiwan to Japan with no friends except the plants and trees? Could a madman have returned to Bombay with no passport and secured a courtyard and attached building with wondrous hydroponic gardens? asked Iqbal with a sweeping gesture of his hand.

The hydroponics were truly wondrous, and as I looked at the tomato that was still sitting there on the ground where I had dropped it, I could not help but agree with my brother in life. If this Netaji was a madman, then perhaps being mad is better than not being mad, or at least it is more useful as a means to accomplishing great and wondrous things. And so I was once again drawn into agreement with my brother Iqbal, and once again I felt our wavelengths connect together, and I even understood that sometimes you may have to lie in the interest of the truth, at least in foreign relations affairs. Finally I decided to leave alone the matter of me spending all our years of brotherhood not knowing that Iqbal's mother's side of the family was Pakistani. That question could wait until later. For now I needed to understand what foreign relations task we were assigned to do.

We are to liaison with representatives of three different Pakistani groups, said Iqbal, and hand over a shipment of hydroponic onions.

But we cannot go to Pakistan, I said in protest, my wife will be angry if I am not home soon.

No no, said Iqbal, we are not going to Pakistan.

By deductive reasoning I quickly arrived at the alternative.

Which means those Pakistani lussuns are coming here to Mumbai, I said.

Liaisons, said Iqbal, lussun means garlic.

17

But why us, I asked, does Netaji not already know these people and have relations with them?

No, said Iqbal, these are new people.

So then all the more reason for Netaji to meet them and develop new relations with them, I said.

Yes, said Iqbal, but they will not deal directly with Netaji.

Why not, I asked.

Because they are extremists, said Iqbal, and so they will only deal with a Muslim.

Now it all became clear to me: Netaji's questioning of Iqbal's religion and background, the meaningful glances, the pat on the shoulder. And as I thought about all that, my previous brainwave returned and I realized we were in a supremely advantageous position to seize the hydroponic shipment and distribute the onions to the onionless crowds of Mumbai. We would be true heroes, and the names of RK and Iqbal would ring out through the streets as onion bhajias and other wondrous derivatives of onion were cooked and consumed. Perhaps there would even be a special day named after us, and every year the people would honor us by having onion-based festivals and fairs across the city of Mumbai and maybe even including the suburbs of Mumbai, depending on how large the shipment of onions turned out to be.

How large is the shipment of onions, I asked.

Five thousand kilos, said Iqbal.

I almost fell off my chair with weight-shock. Five thousand kilos is a tremendous and wondrous amount of anything, let alone onions during a time of onion problem and possible onion crisis. Now I understood why all of these onions had to be under lock and key, and why Netaji could not let silly buggers like myself run free through the Mumbai streets until trust had been gained. I laughed to myself when I realized that Netaji was right not to trust me, because I would shortly be proving myself untrustworthy in the task of delivering five thousand kilos of onions to these bearded terrorists. I laughed again, and when I emerged from my brainwave, Iqbal was eyeing me suspiciously.

You are acting funny, he said.

No no, I said.

You are not planning any funny business I hope, said Iqbal.

Can there be any funnier business plans than delivering five thousand kilos of onions to Pakistani extremist groups? I said in hopes of diverting the question without actually answering it.

Yes, said Iqbal, if you hope to divert the onion shipment

from the Pakistani militants to the Mumbaikars, it would count as funny business.

But Iqbal, I said.

Iqbal looked shocked. I rarely call him by name, partly because I am always near to him when talking, and so I just talk and he knows I am talking to him.

But Iqbal, I said again, how can we give away the crisp onions to a bunch of foreigners when our Mumbai brothers and sisters are without the same?

That is not for us to question, said Iqbal, our government does that anyway through exports and other such trade agreements.

So you do not want to question it, I said, just accept it?

Now this hit Iqbal like a squirrel being hit by a samosa. He was quiet for many moments, and I could tell that he was thinking about the question and its relation to our aggressive stance on the truth and its pursuit. After many more moments of quiet thought, Iqbal finally looked directly at me, and immediately I knew that my brother in life was fully back on my wavelength.

You are correct, he said, all this talk about onion reducing border conflict and what-not may be true, but we cannot simply accept the truth based on someone saying so. We will have to find out for ourselves first, and only then will we allow the shipment of onions to be delivered.

18

But how to find out for ourselves without transporting ourselves personally to the borders or even the interior provinces of Pakistan and interviewing the villagers? Of course, we would be up to the task—up north they speak only Hindi and Urdu, and we have good command over those two sister languages. But the problem is with the transportation and the explanation to our wives and also visa requirements for Pakistan, which can be problematic for common Indians.

We will have to question the liaisons themselves, said Iqbal firmly.

What? I said, but that could be dangerous.

Perhaps, said Iqbal, but nobody said pursuit of the truth is a safe thing to do.

No, I said, in fact, if anything, they say the opposite.

And this thought curdled my blood and bothered my digestive tract. After all, pursuit of truth led to Gandhiji's untimely death at the hands of the villain Godse. And Iqbal and I were not as good in truth pursuit and not as noble and great as Gandhiji, so what hope would we have against villains with beards and AK47s?

Will they have AK47s? I asked Iqbal.

But now Netaji had re-entered the room, and he laughed when he heard my question.

I see Iqbal has explained some of the plans but maybe not all of the details, he said.

I looked at Iqbal and then at Netaji and then at the empty plate that once held the Bombay-duck. The plate was yellow and greasy, and perfectly reflected my state of mind and stomach at that crucial juncture in my life.

Not to worry, said Netaji, the people you will meet are not murderers, they simply work for murderers.

But is the servant of a terrorist-murderer also not a terrorist-murderer? I asked, just like the servant of a madman must necessarily be a madman himself.

At this last statement Bhatkoo eyed me from through the door, but I think he was smart enough to know that a reaction from him would simply prove my point and expose him as a madman-servant of a madman-master. I felt good at my psychological manipulation, and this gave me some confidence when I thought about how I could use the same powers to extract data and other information from the servants of the bearded Pakistani terrorists.

And technically speaking, the groups scheduled to meet

us tomorrow are not yet murderers, said Netaji, since they are newly formed and have not made any attacks yet.

Iqbal nodded and looked at me in earnest as if to apologize for not making this all-important point.

I scratched myself and thought aloud. So they are terrorists in name only and not yet in deed and action, I said wisely.

Correct, said Netaji, and you two, with a successful exchange of onions for weapons, can extend their period of philosophical-but-not-physical terrorism.

Exchange? I said, again looking at Iqbal, who was now shifting about and looking up at the ceiling and then down at the tiles.

Correct, said Netaji, you will give them onions, and they will give you weapons, and they will take the onions back to Pakistan, and you both will expunge the region of such weapons by dropping them into the Arabian Sea.

Now Iqbal seemed very excited. He looked at me with a nodding head, and to tell the truth, I was excited as well. This was really good foreign relations work, something that truly was making some physical impact while ignoring the philosophical impact, which is important, since most foreign policy focuses on silly philosophical things while allowing people to get shot and raped and burned and what-not. This Netaji may be a madman and is probably not even really Netaji, but no one can deny his diplomacy and foreign policy wisdom at this point.

Still, the presence of weapons would make it dangerous work nonetheless, and so I proceeded with caution, and tried to use my powers of reverse psychological manipulation.

But tell me one thing Netaji, I said, will the guns and weapons be active and loaded?

Perhaps, said Netaji, even though I have asked for bullets and bomb-detonators to be delivered in a separate boat, you never know with terrorist groups that you have not worked with before.

Boat? I asked. What boat?

The boat that will carry the Pakistanis and the guns and the bombs from Pakistan, said Netaji. How else to bring them here? By bullock-cart through the Himalayas? Or by aeroplane and parachute? You are quite a silly bugger. It is good that Iqbal will be leader of the exchange operation.

Iqbal seemed to take this as his cue to step up to me and explain the previously unexplained details of this highly dangerous and complicated mission. Apparently at this very moment Netaji's attendants were loading up two boats with onions. Iqbal and me and Bhatkoo and one more attendant would be operating those boats, and we would be meeting two equivalent-sized boats in the dark waters beyond the Haji Ali darga. After exchanging codewords and pleasantries, we would effect an exchange of boats, and once the Pakistanis had taken the onion-boats away to the high seas, we were to sink the two gun-boats and return to shore as secret heroes and full members of Netaji's Hydroponic Foreign Policy Institute.

So we are to sink the gun-boats and swim back to the Haji Ali darga? I asked Iqbal. In the water? In the dark? Are you mad? Have you become a madman also?

No no no, said Netaji with a laugh. There will be another

boat of mine that will come and meet you once the Pakistanis have gone. You will begin the sinking procedure, and then you will all be evacuated to the third boat and brought back to the Indian Motherland like secret heroes whose names nobody will know because our work must be kept secret.

But can I tell my wife, I said.

No no no, said Netaji, that could cause problems.

Why? I said.

I do not know your particular wife, said Netaji with his head bowed, and so I do not want to generalize, but many wives have a tendency to bring up practical obstacles to such plans as exchange of boats in the darkness and sinking two boats with thousands of kilos of guns and bombs and bullets and detonators.

I thought about my wife and realized that perhaps she would point out some difficulties in the plan, and perhaps even try and persuade me to abort the plan and go to the police or the Navy or the Coast Guard.

I see, I said quietly, I see.

Good, said Netaji, good. This will happen tomorrow night, and so now you both can go home to your particular wives, but Bhatkoo and one more attendant will accompany you.

19

As we walked home, I noticed it was starting to get dark, and I remembered that I had not telephoned my wife to tell her I'll not be home for lunch. But now it was already getting close to dinner time, so this could be a problem. And to top that off, I had to somehow explain why this Bhatkoo chap is accompanying me and staying in our house for one night and one day.

I looked at my mobile phone and wondered why my wife had not called me. But then I realized that the mobile signal must not have been available in that dark hole of Netaji's, and this was confirmed when I saw the voicemails and the text-mails that were inquiring on my lunch status at first and then overall status. So I quickly telephoned my wife.

Hello baby, I said in a happy tone, I am coming home now.

The wife was not happy, but she is a nice lady and she will not shout at me over the phone, and so the conversation was short enough and pleasant enough. Still, the problem of the Bhatkoo explanation remained, and I wondered what to do. I looked at Iqbal, the answer-man, and I realized that his problem of the day had at least been solved. He was still clutching the packet of onions, and it appeared he was having a pleasant conversation with the other attendant, the one I presumed would stay with him to keep watch and make sure no secrets were told and no Coast Guard was informed.

What will you tell your wife about this man? I asked Iqbal as I pointed at the other attendant.

You mean Shamoo? Iqbal asked, indicating that the other attendant was named Shamoo.

Yes Shamoo, I said impatiently.

What to tell? said Iqbal. The wife will not be meeting Shamoo, so there is nothing to tell.

Why, I said, will he not be staying with you to keep watch?

No, said Bhatkoo with a smirk, we are both assigned to you only for tonight.

I looked at Bhatkoo and then at Shamoo, who at this point was showing a smirk of his own. I held my head and then my stomach, and I shook both head and stomach. It seemed like tonight would be more dangerous and stressful than tomorrow night.

Not to worry, said Shamoo suddenly and loudly, we have brought our own food and our own bedrolls, and so we'll not cause much maintenance and trouble for you and your wife and any others who may be in your flat.

There are no others presently, I said, because my children are staying in college hostels.

Then it will be no problem at all, said Shamoo, we will eat while sitting on the floor, and we will sleep by placing the bedrolls on the floor, and it will be like we are not even there.

But what will I tell my wife? I said with annoyance. How to explain you two buggers eating and sleeping on my floor suddenly?

That is your problem, said Bhatkoo.

No, I said loudly, it is your problem as well. My wife is a smart woman, and some weak story will not pass muster in my flat. If the story is not strong, she will ultimately find out the truth, and more than likely I will be beaten and you both will be arrested and all the boats will be intercepted by the Coast Guard tomorrow night.

This seemed to worry Bhatkoo and Shamoo, and they looked at each other and then at Iqbal and then at me and then at the ground and then up at the darkening sky. At this point they could have easily made threats of violence, but since they did not, I understood that these people were not violent sorts and would not try any kind of strong-arm tactics. Perhaps Netaji was correct when he said that one could say he too is a Gandhian.

Never mind it then, said Bhatkoo with a defeated sound in his voice, we will both sleep on the road outside your building tonight.

But then my Gandhian heart became a little bit soft and I shook my head.

No, I said, that will not do. If we are all to risk life and dryness together on the Arabian Seas tomorrow night, then it is only right that you sleep comfortably inside my flat tonight. I will make up some story, and if I get some beatings, then I will take them like a Gandhian.

At hearing this, Bhatkoo looked at me with a respect that I had not seen in his previous expressions that day towards me, and I thought that perhaps I had won him over with my staunch adherence to the Gandhian principle of staunch adherence. After all, did Gandhiji himself not say that first they will laugh at you, and then you will win?

20

But victory was not to be won so easily by me, even though there had been no shortage of people who had laughed at me on this first day of our Gandhian adventures. The wife was not happy to see me come late, and as she began to shout at me for causing her some worry, she noticed the unannounced house guests and so she had to put on a smiley face and pull back her shouting, which made her more angry in the way that only I can tell. And in all this I had not even thought of a good story to tell her, but that is just as well, because who am I to think I can get away with lying to my dearest wife? I cannot, and so I subconsciously knew it is better to not say anything than to say something that is not true, because the latter way will lead only to shoutings and beatings for me. And so I was concise and business-like in my dealings with dearest wife that night.

It is an important matter of business, I told her privately in the kitchen, and I cannot explain it all currently because it is complicated.

So I am a simpleton wife who cannot understand complicated matters of business, is it? she asked me.

No baby, I said, you know that it is me who is the simpleton in this family, and so it will give me a headache to try and explain it, and even if I explained it, it is not so interesting and you will possibly fall asleep while I explain, and I do not want you to fall asleep so quickly tonight, baby.

Why not, she said with a smile.

You know why not, I said with a smile and a nudge.

But what of your business colleagues, she asked, what if they hear us?

We will keep the TV on in the bedroom and they will not hear anything, I said.

The wife giggled and pushed me out of the kitchen, and I went back to the living room pleased at my double-victory. Not only had I handled the Bhatkoo-Shamoo situation without too much falsehood, but I would also be getting little bit of bedroom action. Good, I thought, because perhaps this will be the last time I see my beloved wife.

And this moment was the first time I truly contemplated the danger and madness of what we would be attempting the following night in the Arabian Sea beyond the sacred island that contains the Haji Ali darga. And although by now I was confident that Netaji and his people were not of violent nature, this actually caused more worry, because what is the use of having nonviolent people with you if the opposing group is bent on inflicting violence on the high seas?

The worry was showing on my face when I walked towards the spare room where Bhatkoo and Shamoo were preparing their bedrolls.

RK-sahib, said Bhatkoo in a compassionate tone that I had not heard before, you do not need to worry. We are there, no? Nothing bad will happen to you and your friend Iqbalji. We have been given strict instructions that the personal safety of you two is more important than the personal safety of us two, and the safety of us four is paramount compared to any thoughts of onions or guns or bombs or bullets or detonators. If the situation goes bad, we have a perfect exit plan that cannot fail under any circumstance.

Wonderful, I said with relief.

Bhatkoo and Shamoo looked at each other and smiled proudly, and I got the feeling that they had done similar operations before, and so perhaps they were correct and there would be no danger of lifelessness, although danger of wetness would certainly be there.

So what is the exit plan, I asked casually.

Ah no no no no, said Bhatkoo with that same old smirk once more.

Ay na na na na, said Shamoo with his own variation of that madman's smirk.

What? I asked.

We cannot tell you the emergency exit plan, said Bhatkoo, because the plan is too good.

So good, said Shamoo, that if you learn of it you may decide to use it even if it is not an emergency situation.

Remember, said Bhatkoo, you are not fully trustworthy yet.

I nodded in agreement and took my leave of the two of them, but not before I invited them to join me and my wife for dinner at the table. With great gratefulness and huge humility they both declined and said they would eat their packed dinner in the room and sleep soon.

We are just servants, said Bhatkoo, and not fit to be eating at the table with your honorable wife.

Nonsense, I said, do not talk like that in the house of a Gandhian.

Why, said Shamoo, do your regular servants sit at the table and eat breakfast and drink tea with you and your wife?

No, I said with some discomfort, but those servants are employed by me and this is their workplace so I have a different relation with them.

Fine, said Bhatkoo, perhaps someday we will join you and your wife at the table.

But not today, said Shamoo.

Fine, I said as I took my leave, sleep well then and do not hesitate to wake me if there is an emergency.

Then as I walked away I remembered something and looked back at them.

But please knock on the bedroom door and wait for me to open it if such a situation arises, I said quickly as I thought about my wife and the TV.

21

The TV was still on when I awoke the next morning, the morning of the second day of our Gandhian adventures. I sat up immediately and looked at the time because I was worried about being late for work. After all, I had already missed the previous day due to imagined bus problem, and I could not miss another day. Anyway, today was Saturday, and even though Saturday has always been a full working day in India, things are changing in the Indian office culture nowadays and so it is becoming less of a working day. Still, I had to at least show my bulbous face at the office for a few hours, and I also wanted to get out of the house and not have to face my wife and any more detailed questions about how come I have work colleagues staying with me but I am missing work for two days in a row.

I took bath and dressed myself and only then went to check

and see if Bhatkoo and Shamoo were awake and ready. Their room was empty when I arrived, and for a second I hoped that the previous day was all a dream induced by not eating proper lunch. But as I became convinced that it was indeed a dream, I experienced the funny feeling of sadness, like I was sad that it was a dream. That could only mean one thing: I was becoming a true Gandhian and becoming addicted to the aggressive pursuit of passive resistance.

Fooled you, came a voice from the ceiling.

Yes yes, came another voice from another part of the ceiling.

I looked up to see Bhatkoo and Shamoo suspended from different-different parts of the same ceiling. After rubbing my eyes to make sure it was not another dream like how sometimes in a dream you dream of other things, I examined the situation and found that it was not as fantastical as I had previously supposed. Bhatkoo and Shamoo were individually suspended by long cloths and bedsheets that they had affixed to large hooks that I had once used to hang a very large swing. I do not know why they had decided to do such a silly thing, but at least it was clear to me that their doing so was not a sign of the supernatural and more likely a sign of the mental instability of these poor servants who may have spent too much time in a dark hydroponic hole doing strange things for a one-hundred-year-old madman with the skin of a soap model.

We saw the hooks and could not resist, said Bhatkoo as he lowered himself and then went to help Shamoo come down without incident.

Yes, I said, the hooks are indeed unresistable.

Both of them laughed, and they were pleased when I offered them fresh tea and some hot toast and butter and jam. It seemed that they had not packed any food for breakfast.

We finished breakfast, and although I offered to allow use of my spare bathroom for them to bathe, they said it would not be necessary at that point, and they would bathe later at the hydroponics headquarters. Of course, I informed them that I would have to go to office for at least three-to-four hours, but they laughed and said not to worry about office because Netaji has taken care of it already.

Means what? I asked in worry, fearing that Netaji has sent some madman to my office to relieve me of my hard-earned office job.

Not to worry, said Bhatkoo, Netaji will explain when we arrive at his place.

What about Iqbal? I said.

Iqbalji already knows that Netaji has engineered a release from Saturday work for you both, said Shamoo, and so he will meet us near the pao-bhaji-walla shortly, and we will all walk to the courtyard where Netaji must be finishing up his sweeping duties by now.

I felt a small bit of worry with mention of the pao-bhaji-walla. After all, it was due to fleeing from the pao-bhaji-walla that we first came across the previously undiscovered courtyard of Netaji's. In some way it seemed fitting that our second day of Gandhian adventures also begins with a sighting of the pao-bhaji-walla, and perhaps it would not be so bad to eat a few quick plates of his special bhaji before starting this day.

And Netaji says that you are not to eat any pao-bhaji, said Bhatkoo as if my thoughts were available for all to read.

Why not, I demanded.

Because of danger of sea-sickness later, said Shamoo.

Yes, said Bhatkoo, today you will be on a strict diet prepared in the house of Netaji.

Although this troubled me, as any talk of others restricting my diet troubled me, I did not argue, because now I was a seasoned Gandhian, and I expected some hardships and sacrifices to line my path to the truth.

Fine, I said, no pao-bhaji then.

Luckily Iqbal was already near the pao-bhaji stand so we did not have to wait there, and luckily there was a surprising number of people eating pao-bhaji so early in the morning. But as we walked past the stand and towards the main road, the pao-bhaji-walla's helper caught sight of me and came running to me with the pieces of his bucket that I had broken the previous day. At first I thought to run, then I decided to stand and fight, but soon I realized that neither was necessary because the pao-bhaji-walla himself had called his helper back and ordered him to leave me alone.

My eyes met the wise eyes of the pao-bhaji-walla, and he gave me a look of respect and recognition, and then I saw his eyes move past me and settle on Bhatkoo. The pao-bhaji-walla nodded at Bhatkoo as if there was some secret knowledge that existed between the two of them, and then soon that entire scene was over and we were once again standing in the courtyard that was swept clean of all dirt and dust and other particles of rubbish that you see even on the cleanest of Mumbai's streets.

Netaji was nowhere to be seen. Now again I started to wonder if even though Bhatkoo and Shamoo were real, perhaps Netaji was a dream. Just as I was vowing to myself to start eating a meal in between breakfast and lunch to reduce risk of hallucination and daytime dreams, Netaji sprung into action from behind one pillar of his building.

Aha RK-sahib, he said with a fresh-faced smile, and Iqbalji.

Good morning, I said with some mixed feelings.

Hello, said Iqbal with some other feeling.

Come, said Netaji, let us go inside and talk about the plan for tonight.

But it is still nice here and not too warm yet, I said in a hope to stall the descent into this madman's hole once more. Although I admit I was somewhat excited about our plans for the evening, mostly I was scared, and some delay when you are scared is simply natural, is it not?

Nothing to be scared about, said Bhatkoo, we are there, no?

I looked at him and Shamoo, and even in spite of their morning display of mental instability, I believed that they were serious about providing for the safety of myself and Iqbal, my brother in life. And while their morning display may have indicated mental instability, it also indicated physical stability of equal proportions, and if there was some funny business to occur on the high seas this night, then physical stability would be more important to have than mental stability, I thought. And so I smiled and proceeded with the group of my new friends back into the deep dark hole with the hydroponics and what-not.

The place smelled little different today, and immediately I inquired as to the cause of this difference. Iqbal of course looked at me with that look that said why are you asking irrelevant questions at a time like this, but now I was comfortable with my safety and so I felt free to ask questions that may or may not be relevant. And sometimes of course you will not know if a question is relevant until you hear the answer, is that not correct?

Very observant, said Netaji with a smile.

Yes, said Bhatkoo.

The onions have been taken away and packed, said Netaji, and so there is no longer the sweet subversive smell of the onion in this building anymore.

Ah yes, I said while looking at Iqbal with victory in my eyes.

But soon I remembered that it was Iqbal and myself who would be smelling of sweetness and subversiveness today and tonight, because as we had decided, we would have to find a way to question the terrorist liaisons to determine for ourselves whether this onion exchange was really preventing violence at the borders and in the villages and towns where violence is a daily thing. As we gathered in the sitting area and Netaji was occupied in talking to Bhatkoo and Shamoo, I reminded Iqbal of our subversive plan.

But, said Iqbal, if we are exchanging onions for weapons and then destroying the weapons, is that not proof enough that violence will be reduced?

I think you are losing some of your Gandhian aggressiveness, I said, and perhaps you are not eating enough breakfast in the morning.

Why you say that, asked Iqbal.

Because, I said, elimination of some guns and bombs may not automatically reduce violence because we do not know the total number of guns and bombs these groups possess. And also they may use other weapons like spears and swords and large stones.

So what you want to do, said Iqbal, ask them to hand over all the large stones from Pakistan?

Now I was sure that Iqbal had not eaten properly because he was being very short on both temper and patience. So for now I let it go, but internally I had already decided that if questioning indicates that the onions will not serve to reduce the fighting-spirit within the terrorist groups themselves, then we would have to turn the tables on the high Arabian Seas and sink the gun-boats and also take back the onion boats so that the onions can be distributed to the Mumbaikars for bhajias and pakoras and samosas and other savory onion-flavored things.

Then a brainwave hit me that if these terrorist liaisons return to Pakistan having lost the gun-boats but not gained the onion-boats, then perhaps they themselves would be in danger of being violated by their violent leaders. At first that did not seem too bad to me. But then I remembered that the whole point of Gandhian nonviolence is to follow the nonviolent principle when faced with violent people. That is how you win.

But Netaji interrupted my brainwave just then, leaving me in a state of confusion about the soundness of my subversive plan for the evening.

Now remember, said Netaji as he pointed at a nautical chart of the Mumbai coastline, the Haji Ali darga will be your beacon in the dark and so all bearings must be taken in relation to it.

The Haji Ali darga, for those of you that do not know it, is a beautiful structure that looks little bit like a mosque because of domes and minarets, but is actually just a memorial site for a Muslim holy man called Haji Ali who supposedly died in those waters. The building was built on a small rock island some distance away from the mainland, and the way to get there is via a long stone walkway that stretches through the sea itself. Thousands and thousands of Indians and foreigners walk along this walkway every day to visit the darga and pay respects and in return they receive fulfillment of whatever wish they ask for. Of course, the wish has to be somewhat reasonable, I think. You cannot ask to be given wings and be allowed to fly. But who knows with such things. This is India after all, and such things as human flight is sometimes rumored.

But anyway, according to our plan, the onion boats would be pushed off from the mainland within sight of the Haji Ali darga. We would take the boats about one hundred meters beyond the darga, which is safe enough that late-night visitors would not see our boats, but we would still be able to see the bright white, yellow, and green lights from the Haji Ali rock island. We would remain quietly there in the dark until we see the light of the Pakistani gun-boats. They would flash a particular code signal with the light, and we would return the flash with a different code signal. It would be a classic maritime meeting plan, and as we went through the details again and again in order for it to be committed to memory, I felt excited and confident that the plan would go smooth, and perhaps there would not be any need for subversion after all, and we would just make the exchange, sink the gun-boats, and transfer ourselves to the third boat that Netaji would send later.

But then later as we were all eating lunch back upstairs under some shade near the courtyard, Iqbal came up to me with a look that I immediately took to be of aggression and subversiveness, but all directed towards the pursuit of the truth.

Perhaps you are correct, he said, and we will need to conduct our own questioning and pass judgment on the high seas itself and then aggressively take action along the true path.

I smiled as I thought about the perfect balance between myself and Iqbal, my brother in life. When I am aggressive, he is passive, and when I become passive, his aggressiveness comes to the front like a squirrel chasing a samosa.

I nodded in agreement and said nothing because there was nothing more to be said at that point. After my most recent brainwave I had realized that the possibilities were endless, and so speculating on the possible truths was pointless. The only thing that mattered was the one single simple truth, and that could not be arrived at by speculation but only by manipulation of the psychologies of these terrorist liaisons that we would meet on the high Arabian Seas that night.

22

That evening I stopped by my home to meet my wife, and I told her that tonight I'll be staying at those same colleagues' house in order to complete the last bit of the business matter. My wife was very suspicious, but she did not say anything and simply gave me a look that said if you are up to any funny business, you will be beaten like a dog in the street. Of course, by funny business she was not thinking of funny business with another woman or anything like that. She knows me well enough that such trust is not an issue, especially after the recent resurgence of our bedroom activities. But the trust is not so much there that I will not get involved in something that may later turn out to be quite silly.

In my pre-Gandhian days I had done many silly things which I will not repeat here, but now those days are gone and

I am doing important and sensible things. I almost wanted to tell my sweet wife what I was about to engineer on the high seas, but I thought better of it and quickly left the house before any such information was forthcoming.

We travelled to the Haji Ali area quite early so that we could inspect our boats and make sure we were aware of the mechanics of boat-manipulation. Iqbal and I were to command the leading boat, and Bhatkoo and Shamoo were to be on the second boat. The boats would be attached together with a long and thick rope so that they would not drift far apart. At first I was little bit worried about how Iqbal and myself could handle a big boat with two-thousand-five-hundred kilos of onions, but when I saw the actual boats I understood.

The lead boat was much smaller, and now I understood that it was to make it easier for us to get close to the terrorist lead boat and make the formalities of the exchange in a formal manner. The second boat was quite a monstrous thing, and I was happy that I would not be in command of it. Both boats smelled sweet and fine with onions, and at first I worried that maybe people around us will notice and hijack us before we have even left the mainland. But then I shook my head and decided not to confuse myself with too many different possibilities and to focus only on the task at hand.

I was made to wear a black kurta with black pajamas and black rubber chappals. Iqbal was dressed in a fine black sherwani, and he looked like a truly great and powerful Muslim leader at that point, what with his finely shaped beard and thin Aurangzeb-like face. But then I remembered that Aurangzeb had imprisoned his father and killed all his brothers so that there would be no dispute about who gets to be the king, and so I removed all such historical references from my mind.

Bhatkoo and Shamoo were also dressed in black, but their clothes were little bit older and dirtier, perhaps part of a strategy to make it clear who the leaders were.

We boarded our respective boats, and immediately I was thankful that I had not eaten any special bhaji that morning. I quickly realized that the negative side of the small boat was that it moved this way and that way very easily even in calm seas.

This is why I wanted to come here early, said Netaji, so you get used to standing on this boat as it rocks from side to side.

Yes, said Bhatkoo, very important.

Correct, said Netaji, they must think you are a master of the high Arabian Seas.

Or they will not respect you, said Shamoo.

And without respect, said Bhatkoo, all could be lost.

What nonsense, I said, we do not respect the terrorists, but still we are doing the transaction, and so respect is not a prerequisite for the smooth flow of the onions-for-weapons exchange.

Then you will not do any talking, said Netaji, only Iqbal will speak directly with the terrorists.

What, I said, but Iqbal and I are joint leaders so we must speak jointly.

Now I was worried about how I would conduct my end of the questioning and psychological manipulation if I was not allowed to speak to the terrorists. But how could I lie to Netaji and say that I respect the terrorists when their work of terror is not respectable? By now I had told enough lies in the past two days of the Gandhian adventures, but how much to lie? Somewhere there has to be a limit, and to say I respect anti-India terrorists is too much to stomach while standing on this boat as it moves from side to side.

There must be mutual respect, said Netaji, if the transaction is to go smoothly. Remember, you have a higher purpose of peace and reduction of weapons and hence reduction of violence.

And also, said Iqbal, these people we will encounter are respectable enough and we should be formal and polite with them.

I stared up at Iqbal's Aurangzeb-like face and shook my head not as if to say no but as if to clear the head of any confusion or hearing problems. I could not believe that my brother Iqbal was saying such things. I was disgusted, and luckily it was dark in the area or else people would have seen the disgust on my face. But I could not hide my disgust at this last statement, and so I mentioned it out loud.

I am disgusted that you say these people are respectable enough, I said as I spat on the ground and almost hit Bhatkoo's foot with the spit, when in actuality they are enemies of India and in fact enemies of any country that loves democracy and freedom and peacefulness.

So you think the Pakistani people do not love democracy and freedom and peacefulness? asked Iqbal.

Does not look like it, I said with a sulky voice.

Raj, said Iqbal, you are my brother in life.

I almost fell down from name-shock, because even though I rarely call Iqbal by name, he has never in my memory called me by name. This is because he does not speak as much as I do in general, and when he speaks, there is never any doubt he is addressing me, and even if there is doubt sometimes, he still speaks to me without addressing me by name.

What is it, I said with the same sulky voice but actually I was feeling quite soft and a little bit worried as to the graphic nature of this conversation.

Pakistan is also a democracy, said Iqbal softly, even though it may not be blessed with efficient government and honest politicians like how Mother India is blessed.

Perhaps, I said.

And Pakistanis also love freedom and peacefulness, said Iqbal, and maybe they even love freedom and peacefulness more than we Indians do because they have less of both things in daily life.

Now this hit me in the soft spot that controlled my sulky and disrespectful behavior, and so I began to see his point. It is true that the counter-intuitiveness and manipulation inherent in one's own psychology makes you appreciate the fine things that you do not get to appreciate on a daily basis, just like Iqbal loves the Bombay-duck more because he does not eat it as much as he would like.

Like the Bombay-duck, I said with a crack in my voice that came from the emotion that Iqbal's fine words had given rise to in me.

Yes, said Iqbal.

And he came up to me and gave me a tight hug and we were like two brothers who had crossed the Himalayas together and conquered the great question of how to respect people that the media and movies tells you are evil and must be killed and disrespected. The Gandhian spirit was truly alive in us, and now we would use that spirit to propel this boat of onions past the great old Haji Ali darga and towards our destiny on the high Arabian Seas.

23

So for the next one or two or three hours we inspected the boats and took instruction from Netaji and Bhatkoo and Shamoo on how to operate the extra-quiet electric motor on the lead boat and how to use the light-systems and other basic sea-faring mechanisms. Netaji was quite knowledgeable about boats and water and what-not, and I became even more impressed with this man whom I could no longer call mad, but maybe that was only because I too had made the descent into same madness, and from my new vantage point it all looked sane.

Ah, said Netaji, I wish I was coming with you.

Why don't you come then, I said.

Then who will operate the third boat, he said with a smile, that will pick up all four of you once the Pakistanis have gone and you have commenced the sinking procedure on the gun-boats?

I felt silly for asking, especially since we had gone over the plan again and again and committed every stage of planning to memory so that when execution occurs it is smooth and efficient like Indian Parliamentary Process.

Sorry, I said.

No issue, said Netaji, I was only saying because it has been some time since I have done boating, and I used to do it every day when I roamed free in the wild islands of Japan in the 1950s and 1960s.

So you have not done many overseas transactions like this, I said, and by overseas I mean like how we will be over the seas soon for this transaction.

No, said Netaji with a laugh, most of my onion transactions with bordering countries are done via truck and bullock cart, and then the liaisons load up their own boats and take the onions back home. But now of course there is stricter monitoring of all the potential boat-landings around Mumbai, so these buggers do not want to come all the way in to land.

So this is a pioneering feat we are accomplishing, I said proudly.

Yes indeed, said Netaji, and once you are successful you both will become the leaders of the Onion Delivery Department of the Hydroponic Foreign Policy Institute.

Means what, I said.

Means you will conduct such operations on a regular basis of course, said Netaji as if it was an obvious thing.

But I thought this would be a one-time thing to prove

ourselves and then the work would be done and life would be like normal, I said while looking at Iqbal who once again was dodging my gaze.

But see, said Netaji, once you have proved yourself it would mean you are trustworthy and skilled and therefore highly useful for such procedures and operations.

Okay fine I see, I said, and so it would only be logical for us to continue to do such operations until that point where we are no longer trustworthy or skilled.

Or until you are dead, said Shamoo with a smirk and everyone turned to look at him in surprise.

Means what, I said in fear and even some anger.

Sorry, said Shamoo, I mean dead after many many years and of natural peaceful causes of course.

Okay I see, I said in relief, natural death of course will come because all of us cannot live forever like Netaji.

At this statement there was a sudden quietness even though I meant it like how you make a joke by saying something that is not really a joke but you try and say it in a way that makes it sound like a joke.

It is time, said Netaji immediately.

Yes yes, said Bhatkoo.

Let us mount up and embark, said Shamoo.

We said namaste to Netaji and then took to our lead boat. Carefully I started the electric motor while Iqbal took over the wheel in the wheel-room. And then quietly, in the dark waters of the Arabian Sea, we moved towards what I believed would be the finale of our Gandhian adventures.

24

The finale did not come as soon as expected, and we sat upon our dark boats and bounced up and down on the Arabian Sea for a long time. I could hear Bhatkoo and Shamoo talking on their big boat, but I could not see them, and I could not completely make out what they were saying. The air was nice and salty and moist like the sea itself, and that way I had no problem sitting there because it was a nice atmosphere and even the bouncing did not bother me so much anymore. I felt like a master of the high Arabian Seas already, and I was confident I would command the respect of these Pakistanis when the time of the formalities arrived.

You will have their respect, said Iqbal wisely, because now you have respect for them.

I did not question the recent infusement of Iqbal's tongue

with such inspirational speech because I too was feeling inspired by the atmosphere of the dark gentle waves and the beautiful Haji Ali darga in the distance and the smell of salt and moisture and other things that float in the water around this greatest city of Mumbai. I felt that whatever happened from then on would be fine and acceptable because we had followed our pursuit of Gandhian principles to their logical extreme, and perhaps now even left logic behind and so are following only to the extreme. This analysis struck me as quite incisive but yet funny, and I was about to inform Iqbal of it when we saw the flashing lights in the distance.

Bhatkoo was the official light-code reader, but due to good planning, all of us had memorized the lighting codes, and I could immediately tell that these lights were indeed belonging to the Pakistanis.

I stood up and began to move about the boat due to tension in my stomach and legs and heart, but the steady hand of Iqbal, my brother in life, steadied me like he had steadied me many times before, and I stood still and awaited our Gandhian encounter with the Pakistanis. As the lights came closer, I picked up the big flashlight and handed it to Iqbal, who was the official light-code-dispatcher just like Bhatkoo was the official light-code-reader.

The Pakistanis changed their light-code, which was the sign that they had seen our light-code and were zooming in to our location in the dark seas. Soon we could see the outlines of two big boats highlighted against the blue-black sky of the Mumbai night. It was a sight that I will never forget: the boats were big and dark and of wooden frames with big posts and dark-looking sails that flip-flapped in the warm moist wind of the Arabian Seas. At the head of the lead boat stood two Pakistanis. They were tall Pathani men in their black Pathani suits and one of them had a big flowing beard and I could not see the other one's face.

The bearded Pakistani raised his hand and I raised my hand to wave to him, but Iqbal stopped me.

He is not waving to you, said Iqbal, he is instructing his men to cut their motor so his boat does not bash into our boat and cause an accident.

But just then the bearded Pakistani waved to me, and I felt like I was master of the high seas after all.

See, I told Iqbal, they already respect me as is evidenced by the return of my wave.

But then we realized that both of us were wrong when we saw the other terrorist gun-boat approaching us silently from the other side. It was the other boat that this bearded man was waving to, and I was suddenly sure that it was the signal to attack with great immediacy and extreme prejudice. Only then did I think of the silliness of meeting terrorists in the dark when large amounts of scarce commodities were to be exchanged for large amounts of weapons with the weapons starting off in the possession of the terrorists. Only then did I become certain that it was only logical for the terrorists to simply kill us and then go back to Pakistan with the onions and also the weapons. And then I thought why would they even bring the weapons when they could simply fill their boats with thousands of kilos of live terrorists and perhaps even launch a fresh attack on Mumbai.

I told all this to Iqbal very quickly as we watched the second boat in fear.

Not to worry, he said, we must put forth our trust and these people will prove themselves trustworthy.

But I could tell that even Iqbal, the answer-man, was little bit at a loss for concrete and stable answers as our doom seemed to be getting closer and closer with each gentle wave. I stared at the Haji Ali darga in the distance, and I silently made a vow that I'll not do anything again without full knowledge and approval of my dear wife if only I can be saved from this one last silly thing I have engineered myself into doing.

Now the first boat was almost touching our boat, and the bearded Pakistani put one leg on our boat and threw a thick Pakistani rope from his boat to ours, binding the two boats together so we cannot escape. The Pakistani now looked at us, and only then did I see that he looked a little bit nervous.

Greetings, he said, I am Yoosuf.

As we had been instructed by Netaji, Iqbal was to be the first to speak due to concern for the extremists' extreme religious sensibilities.

Salaam Alaykum, Iqbal said with a respectful gesture that looked like he had practiced it before.

Alaykum Salaam, said Yoosuf with a similarly graceful gesture.

Hello hello, I said in what I thought was a respectful tone, but due to my own nervousness my voice was actually very loud and squeaky, like when a squirrel is choking on a samosa.

Yoosuf looked at me and smiled in happiness.

You seem to be a funny bugger, he said, like Veeru who is my brother in life.

Yoosuf looked past my shoulder and then I turned to see a somewhat bulbous Pakistani on the second boat. He was smiling and bobbing his head in time to the boat-bobbing, and it was quite comical and I could not help but smile.

Yes yes I am Veeru, he said with a smile.

But you are Hindu, I blurted out without thinking.

Iqbal poked me hard now, but what was said had been said, and now we had to deal with the aftermath.

Yoosuf laughed once more.

Yes, he said, Veeru is certainly Hindu.

Yes yes, said Veeru, my entire mother's side of the family is from Indian Punjab.

How funny, I said, because the mother's side of Iqbal's family is from Pakistani Punjab.

At this everyone laughed a little bit, and it was like how we say the laddoo has been split up and shared to make peace via sharing of sweetmeats.

How nice, I said, because we were told you are extremists who will only deal with Muslims and so in fact I was even hesitant to speak up.

Now Yoosuf pulled on his beard and took on a very serious and quite scary expression.

Make no mistake, he said, we are extremists.

And actually I live in constant fear for my life, said Veeru, as they could chop me up and discard me anytime without warning due to their extremist nature.

But you said he was your brother in life, I said in protest

but in that same squeaky loud voice. You would kill your own brother in life?

All the more proof of our extremism, said Yoosuf.

And suddenly all the laughter and lightness of the bobbing had turned into seriousness and heaviness, and now the bobbing felt like I was being shaken by the gods that had undoubtedly taken old Haji Ali's life in the first place. Again my fear of death came to the forefront, and I looked around to see if Bhatkoo and Shamoo were close by, but their boat was quite far, although still attached to ours by rope. According to instructions that Netaji claimed to have received directly from the terrorist cell phone, our second boat was only to approach after the initial formalities had been formalized.

Then time for chit-chat is over, said Iqbal in a loud and commanding voice that I was surprised to hear, and let us do the exchange and move on with our respective pursuits in life.

And in afterlife, I said without thinking.

At this careless statement of mine Yoosuf and Veeru looked at each other across our boats, and although it was dark and I could not be sure, I really thought they both looked scared for one minute.

Where are the onions? shouted Veeru from behind me.

And now when I heard that Veeru's voice had taken on a similar squeaky tone like that of a Pakistani mountain rat choking on a kabaab, I began to get some confidence like how when you are facing death you are able to call upon senses and sensibilities that otherwise do not come out of your being. And so I regained my composure and replied in a loud and deep voice that surprised everyone including me.

They are in the boats of course, I said, where else do you think? In our pockets? Five thousand kilos of onions we will put in our pockets or what? Now deliver us the weapons without delay. We have many other things to do tonight and we cannot just sit here on the high seas and waste time with you squeaky mountain rats.

At this even Yoosuf seemed to hesitate, but I could tell he was a confident man and leader of other less-confident men, and so his hesitation, if any, did not last long.

Come on board, he said, but leave your weapons behind.

At this I looked at Iqbal and Iqbal looked at me.

Yes fine, I said quickly so as not to dwell on the topic and expose the fact that we had no weapons of note.

But since we did not remove any weapons from our persons, it would appear as if we had not left our weapons behind. And so as we stepped on board Yoosuf's boat, he quickly patted our backs and sides as if to check for secret weapons. When he was bending down, I could see one more of his men standing on his boat, and that man certainly had something that could only be an AK47 assault rifle, the gun of choice for terrorists due to long-term contracts with the Russian manufacturers of said weapons. I thought back to the long-time alliance of India and Russia, and for a moment I lamented the fact that our peace-loving government had not negotiated a special rate for AK47s for our people as well so that we would be armed when doing such dangerous exchanges.

No weapons? said Yoosuf in surprise while looking at his henchman and then Veeru and then me and then his henchman again.

It must be a trap, shouted Veeru from across the boats, their boats must be set with timer bombs to kill us once the exchange is made. We were told to take extreme care when dealing with these dangerous Indian extremists, and now we are finished, Yoosuf. I told you not to be so trusting. Now they will kill us and my wife will be alone and my children will grow up without a father.

Now I lost my cool as well because of the darkness and the bobbing and the shouting and everything, and so I began yelling also.

No, I shouted, it is you buggers who have set the trap with your AK47s and beards, and now it is my wife who will live as a widow and it is only because of our mistake of trusting you and not bringing our weapons.

I was about to go on and on, but Iqbal raised his hand to stop me. He gave me a look that said to be quiet, and then he turned to Yoosuf, who seemed quite calm at this point, possibly because he had ownership of all known guns and bombs and beards except for Iqbal's small pointy beard.

We have no weapons, said Iqbal, because we have come here to do an honorable exchange that will further the goals of both our groups.

Yoosuf nodded and looked at his henchman and then passed Veeru a look similar to the calming look that Iqbal had delivered to me.

No need for shouting and high tension, said Yoosuf, and let us make this exchange and you can go about your business and we will return to Pakistan with the onions.

Now that things were calming down, I began to remember our secondary goal of psychological manipulation to try and find out if this exchange would truly reduce violence or simply reduce Indian onion supply.

But without these guns, I said, how will you conduct your activities of terrorism?

At this Yoosuf seemed surprised and he looked across at Veeru as if asking his Pakistani Hindu brother for clarification. But instead I decided to clarify.

If you are giving us five thousand kilos of guns and bullets and bombs and detonators, I said, then you must have many more kilos remaining in Pakistan or else you will not be able to conduct terror attacks and border strikes except by use of mountain goats and large stones and maybe spears.

Yoosuf was very quiet, and I wondered if he was about to have us put to death for such probing questions. Finally he looked at me and spoke.

But we are not terrorists, he said.

At this I looked at Iqbal and could tell that even Iqbal was little taken aback. Then I understood Yoosuf's meaning, and I felt very proud of myself for understanding, because it meant that I had truly enabled myself to look at the world from the view and mindset of my enemy. Of course from his point of view he is not a terrorist. He is simply a freedom fighter or a dealer of justice or simply a working-class man whose job is to shoot Indians and blow up things.

I understand, I said proudly, you do not call your killing activities terrorism due to your having a different viewpoint from that of us.

No, said Yoosuf, our activities do not involve any killing of people.

Then I remembered that Iqbal and Netaji had mentioned that these buggers are a new group and so perhaps they have not accomplished their first mass killings or even small-scale killings.

I understand, I said, but you will be killing at some point.

Yes but not people, said Veeru from behind me, only goats and chickens.

I turned to Veeru in confusion, and then back to Yoosuf in surprise. Now I was not sure what to think. Could it be that these buggers are still in training and hence are only murdering and blowing up these small animals that probably do not have AK47s for their own self-defense? But still, if you are to become a professional killer of men, then why not practice on men only? Why kill the goats and chickens?

For the mutton biryani, said Veeru from behind me, and the chicken kabaabs.

Yes, said Yoosuf, we are representatives from the Pakistani Association for Preparation and Serving of Food.

Yes yes, said Veeru, we are cooks.

25

Then why did you tell the Netaji that you are terrorists? I asked.

By this time we had explained that we were not Indian extremists but actually Gandhians, and so the tension had dissolved a little bit. We had entered the small cabin area of the Pakistani lead boat, and we were sitting in close quarters in a dining hall kind of place that smelled very strongly of the wondrous dishes of the Pakistani people.

Because when one of our members tried to arrange the exchange by giving the true name and purpose of our group, said Yoosuf, your leader told us he will only deal with terrorist groups.

I see, said Iqbal.

I nodded. This was indeed consistent with what Netaji said was his strategy. After all, he said that when he provides onions to the angry groups, they become less angry and are hence less likely to inflict angry actions of dissatisfaction against others. Of course, the members of all these angry groups are simply just the villagers from the small towns, and when they receive onions, they pass it on to their families and their groups' cooks.

And that gave me a brainwave.

But where did you get five thousand kilos of guns? I asked suspiciously.

Yoosuf made a sighing noise and looked at the ground.

Yes, he said, many of our cooks are in fact cooks for some militant groups or camps.

Yes, said Veeru, and so we banded together and made a raid of the gun storage places and what-not.

But is that not dangerous for you all, said Iqbal.

Yes, I said, what if they had discovered you in the act?

Then we would have been chopped up and discarded immediately, said Veeru.

Yes, said Yoosuf, because we ourselves are not violent people or even angry people.

These militant groups are the only employers in our villages, said Veeru, and so we only have the choices of being cooks for the militant groups or being soldiers for the militant groups.

Of course, said Yoosuf quite seriously, third choice is to have ourselves and our families simply starve to death in the mountain villages due to no job or money.

But we are not good at these hunger strikes, said Veeru, like your man Gandhi was.

At the mention of Gandhiji I felt proud, because indeed

the great Mahatma secured many concessions and allowances and freedoms by going on hunger strike at great risk to his own life as well as to the life of Kasturba-ben, his noble wife.

Our man Gandhi, said Yoosuf quietly.

Like our man Jinnah, said Iqbal in reciprocation.

I was inspired by this exchange of respectful mentions of the respective godfathers of the Indian and Pakistani nations. In Pakistan the man Jinnah, originally an Indian of course, as are many old Pakistanis due to Pakistan having not existed before 1947, is held in the same regard and esteem as Gandhiji is held in our country of India. Of course, Jinnah was a great Indian freedom fighter as well, and even though all wise scholars of both Indian and Pakistani history will know that the two countries say different-different things about these two great leaders, it is not the place of us humble Gandhians to say which is correct and which is incorrect. The simple truth is there can be no doubt that both are great. Separate, but equal, one might say.

I said all this aloud to our small group of four men—two Indians, two Pakistanis, two Hindus, two Muslims—total four. For once everyone listened without smiling or laughing or calling me a silly bugger or telling me to shut up, and I could feel that I was drawing the strength from the holy rock island on which the Haji Ali darga quietly sat in the night, unmoved by the gentle waves of the high Arabian Seas. It truly was a moment of great magic and wondrousness, and I knew that all these men on this boat were simple people and brotherly in spirit and intention.

Our moment was broken up by the sound of wood striking wood and the loud shouts of what must have been Bhatkoo and Shamoo and the Pakistani henchman with the AK47.

Do not shoot them, I shouted, they are without weapons of note.

Not to worry, said Yoosuf, our guns are not loaded.

But perhaps your henchman will get bullets from the hatch where thousands of kilos of weapons are present for the exchange, I said.

Not to worry, said Veeru with a smile, the guns we have provided do not match with the bullets we have provided.

And the bombs do not match with the detonators, said Yoosuf.

And so, I shouted in delight, due to deductive logic all the remaining guns and bombs and bullets and detonators in the militant group storages back in Pakistan are mismatched and hence unfit for ignition or explosion.

Yes, said Yoosuf.

Yes yes, shouted Veeru in pride.

But then another shout from upstairs made us alert to possible drama outside, and so we had to cut short our celebrations of the smart peace-loving actions of these Pakistani militant cooks of mutton biryani and chicken kabaabs.

When we emerged into the dark starry night we saw that Bhatkoo and Shamoo had brought their boat close by, and now the second onion boat was touching the first onion boat, and Bhatkoo and Shamoo had been deposited on the ground near us and were being held there at gunpoint.

Do not shoot us, said Bhatkoo.

Or only shoot us in the non-vital organs such as kidney or thigh, shouted Shamoo.

Yoosuf instructed his henchman to put down the gun, but the henchman looked very angry and suspicious.

These two were activating some mechanism on that big

onion boat, he said, and I think it must be a timed bomb to kill us once we have left the vicinity.

No no, shouted Shamoo, we would never destroy five thousand kilos of onions like that.

Bhatkoo kicked him as if to shut him up, and now even I grew suspicious because these two chaps were acting like they had been doing some funny business that was unknown to myself and Iqbal.

Show me, said Yoosuf to the henchman.

The henchman pointed to a metallic object that seemed to have some kind of small red blinking light on it. The object was affixed to the side of the large onion-boat, and to me it definitely looked like some kind of device that could possibly be a sign of trickery on the part of Bhatkoo and Shamoo, or perhaps even Netaji.

Now the trust has been broken, shouted Veeru, and we must kill them with our mutton-choppers.

The henchman turned his gun towards me and Iqbal and indicated for us to sit on the ground next to Shamoo and Bhatkoo, but since I knew the gun was not loaded, I was not scared. So I simply ignored him and I started to slap Shamoo and Bhatkoo hard and on the face with extreme prejudice and great immediacy. They shouted and screamed and cried, but I did not stop until Yoosuf and Iqbal together pulled me away from them.

No, said Yoosuf to Veeru after I had been restrained, sometimes you have to maintain trust on the basis of instinct even when trust appears to have been violated. We will sort this out. If it is a bomb, then I do not think these two jokers will want it to detonate while they are close by, so we are okay for now I think.

Unless they are suicide bombers, shouted Veeru.

Yes, said the henchman, you can never tell with these Indians.

I told you they are murderers and extremists, shouted Veeru again, and now I am proven correct.

Stop it, said Yoosuf.

He looked at me and then at Iqbal and then at me again and then away into the distance at the glowing lights of the Haji Ali darga.

I do not think these two leaders knew of this device, he said finally.

Of course we did not, I shouted as if in anger but really it was in relief.

Iqbal did not say anything, but I could tell he was relieved. Or perhaps he simply had faith that the instincts of Yoosuf would ensure that the situation would not escalate to the use of mutton-choppers on us.

So tell us now, said Yoosuf in a stern voice that was more scary than even a fully loaded AK47, what is this device that you have affixed to the boats we are to be leaving in?

Tracker, said Bhatkoo quietly while looking away from everyone's eyes.

Satellite-based tracker, said Shamoo while looking up into the black sky as if to search for a satellite.

For the Coast Guard to track us and arrest us, said Yoosuf with a sigh.

Bhatkoo kept looking down, and Shamoo kept looking up.

Answer him you bloody fools, I shouted.

They remained silent for many more moments, and finally I began to lose my patience.

Bring me one of those mutton-choppers, I said, and I will dislocate some of the non-vital organs of these buggers.

I think Bhatkoo did not believe me, but Shamoo did not know me as well, and plus I must have looked quite impressive in my black kurta-pajama standing there gently rocking as if I was master of the high Arabian Seas. And so Shamoo finally blurted it out.

Maoists, he said quietly.

The Chinese, I shouted in surprise.

And now everyone shouted, more in surprise than anything else, but possibly a little bit of fear as well, because if the Maoists showed up, it was very likely that they would have no such issue of mismatched guns and bullets, and would laugh at our mutton-choppers as they shot us full of tiny holes and dropped us into the Arabian Seas to add to the other floating objects.

26

After some more interrogation under threat of chopping off the non-vital organs of Shamoo, the full plot became clear to us. Netaji had made a double-deal with the Pakistanis and the Chinese. The Maoists had been given the locator codes for the tracking device in exchange for a small finder's-fee that Netaji would reinvest into the hydroponics infrastructure, and once we had successfully completed our exchange and separated from the Pakistanis, the Maoists would arrive and hijack the Pakistanis and take away the onions.

After all, even though China is number one in onion production, they are also number one in onion consumption, and they rely on some exports from India. So when there is onion problem, these poor Maoists suffer the most due to being lower down on the Chinese hierarchy. And since the Maoists are the ones most active along the India-China borders, their suffering is translated into border usurpation and covert strikes.

I understood that Netaji at some level was trying to create a win-win situation for India by using two external parties against one another. From my limited knowledge, this is the number one strategy of foreign policy, and so I could not fault Netaji, who is a self-proclaimed foreign policy man, for engaging in it. And since he believed that these Pakistanis were actually terrorists, perhaps he did not feel so bad about their potential loss of life at the hands of the Maoists. Possibly he even didn't mind if there was a gun battle between the Pakistanis on the onion ships and the Chinese on their gun-ships resulting in an indeterminate outcome. He could maintain tracking of the situation in case both sides got finished off and the onions were left to float freely on the Arabian Seas. Onions spoil only after long time, and with the salt in the air, possibly the onions could float for months without spoiling.

My detailed thinking was interrupted by the scared voice of Bhatkoo. When I looked at him in contempt and expecting him to be fearful of me, I noticed that his fear was not of me.

We must separate ourselves from these onion-boats, he said, because now that the device has been activated, the Maoists will descend upon us with extreme prejudice and fearful immediacy.

Then why did you activate it, I shouted, you bloody fool.

It was a mistake by Shamoo, said Bhatkoo.

I was only trying to fix it on the boat, protested Shamoo, and I did not know that fixing it in place would automatically activate it.

It becomes active the moment it is in direct view of a satellite, said Bhatkoo, that is why we did not fix it on the boat to begin with and instead kept it closed up in a black cloth.

I gave Shamoo one more tight slap on his face, and then I turned to Yoosuf and Iqbal, both of whom seemed to be the answer-men, for answers.

Should we all stay on the gun-boats, I said, and simply abandon the onions?

I think so, said Iqbal, because loss of onions is better than loss of life.

We cannot return to Pakistan without the onions, said Yoosuf softly but with determination.

And we cannot stay on the gun-boats, said Veeru with some hesitation that made me wonder.

Why not? I said.

Because they are already sinking and will be underwater within fifteen minutes, Veeru replied without looking at me directly in the eyeball.

I looked around, and sure enough, the water levels around us were noticeably higher, which meant by deduction that the ship-surface levels were noticeably lower. I stared at Veeru and then at Yoosuf, who nodded in agreement.

Yes, he said, we have unplugged some pre-made holes on the ships that are allowing water into the lower decks of the gun-boats.

But why? I shouted.

Because they assumed we are Indian violent extremists, said Iqbal wisely, and so they did not want us to have possession of so many weapons despite the bullets and detonators being mismatched.

So even you have done some kind of double-deal, I said to Yoosuf without anger and even with some admiration at the Gandhian qualities of the double-deal.

You could say that, said Yoosuf.

Yes, said Veeru, sorry.

No problem, said Iqbal, we understand why you would want to sink us.

In fact, I said with a laugh, our plan was to sink the gun-boats anyway and escape on a third boat that would come after you are gone.

And this gave me yet another brainwave, my third such brainwave of the night, and I immediately jumped up and down and shouted.

Oh but the solution is simple then, I said, we can all escape on Netaji's boat.

Brilliant, said Iqbal, we will just wait on board the onion-boats while the gun-boats sink.

And when Netaji comes, I said, we will all get onto his boat and be saved.

No, said Yoosuf, we cannot leave the onions behind.

We will fight with mutton-choppers if necessary, said Veeru, but we will either win by gaining the onions or lose by losing our lives.

Now I felt we were in a thick situation. On the one hand we had experienced some bonding with these Pakistani cooks and I did not want to leave them for certain death at the hands of the Maoists. On the other hand, I did not want to meet certain death myself at the hands of anyone, let alone some Maoists on the Arabian high seas.

Then it is decided, said Iqbal, we will all stay on the onion boats and face the Chinese together.

My blood became like milk-curds at hearing this, and I wondered how many holes the Chinese bullets would make in me and whether my body would be found near the Haji Ali island and whether people will even know that it is me. One small tear came into my eye as I breathed in the moist salty air and thanked the gods for having a nice life and then cursed some different gods for forcing my life to end like this.

But sirs, came the squeaky voice of Shamoo.

At first we did not pay attention, and I even wanted to slap him a little bit more just to warm up my blood before the final death-battle with the Chinese.

But sirs, said Shamoo a little bit louder.

What is it, I shouted angrily.

But sirs, he said, why do we not simply pull off the tracking device and throw it into the sea and it will sink and then I do not think the battery will work and also I do not think the satellite signal will penetrate the water.

We all stared at Shamoo and then we all looked away, taking care not to look at any other person directly in the eye because we were all too ashamed and embarrassed for not thinking of such a simple solution to the Chinese onion problem. It is funny how the thoughts can so quickly move one to get ready for a death-battle without first considering all the less dramatic options. That is also one characteristic of foreign policy, I believe.

So we simply sent Shamoo to the onion-boat to pluck off the tracker and throw it into the Arabian Sea, which happily swallowed it up like it was doing a service for us.

27

And so, without the Chinese to worry about for the moment, our only immediate problem was that the two gun-boats were sinking quickly beneath our feet. This was solved by all of us vacating said gun-boats and gathering together on the larger of the two onion-boats. One of the Pakistani henchmen stayed on the smaller onion-boat, and soon we had separated ourselves from the Pakistani ships and were floating alone with the onions and the other things that float on the Arabian Seas.

So now we will simply wait for Netaji's boat, I said happily, and then we will take our leave and you fine Pakistanis can transport yourselves back to your biryani-ovens and kabaab-grills.

Yes, said Yoosuf, it is not such a bad result.

How long do you think it will take for Netaji to come for us, I asked Bhatkoo.

Bhatkoo was quiet, and he was simply staring at the Haji Ali darga as if in contemplation or making a wish for something.

Ay Bhatkoo, I shouted, answer.

Netaji is not coming, he said without shifting his gaze from the red and green lights of the mosque-like dome on the Haji Ali island.

I was going to shout some more, but Shamoo began to speak up, and so I listened first as I prepared to shout and perhaps even continue with the slapping of faces.

Actually Netaji had made a triple-deal, said Shamoo.

Yes, said Bhatkoo, and so the gun-boats were never supposed to be sunk.

He said not to tell you because of your simplistic Gandhian tendencies, said Bhatkoo.

And the lack of trust so far, said Shamoo.

Who is the third party, said Iqbal.

Indian government of course, said Bhatkoo.

Who else will buy five thousand kilos of guns and bombs, said Shamoo.

And who else would Netaji sell weapons to, said Bhatkoo.

Netaji is a patriot as you know, said Shamoo.

My brain was hurting from too many brainwaves and too many secret plans being exposed in the darkness.

So we were supposed to bring the gun-boats in to the shore, said Iqbal, and then Netaji would have the guns loaded onto trucks and sold to the Indian government?

No no of course not, said Shamoo, where to get so many trucks and truck drivers?

Yes, said Bhatkoo, the government is to simply come here and take over the gun-boats directly.

But how? I asked.

Via Coast Guard and Navy, said Bhatkoo.

Joint operation, said Shamoo.

Yes, said Bhatkoo, Netaji has already made the arrangements and the contacts.

Okay fine, I said, so instead of Netaji picking us up it will be the Coast Guard or Navy in a bigger boat. No problem. As long as they drop us off on land so I can go home soon to my dear wife. No problem.

Maybe one small problem, said Shamoo softly as if he was scared of more slaps.

What, I said.

What, said Iqbal.

The Coast Guard and Navy will take us to land, said Shamoo, but we will have to be arrested of course.

What, I shouted.

No, said Iqbal.

And Yoosuf and Veeru looked very worried at this point, and I was happy that the henchman on the other boat was not following the conversation, otherwise the drama would have gotten out of hand.

It is just for public opinion and newspaper coverage, said Bhatkoo, and so there is no need to worry.

Yes, said Shamoo, because Netaji has many government contacts that will see to it that we are freed after some weeks or months.

After the media attention has gone down, said Bhatkoo.

We will have our photographs in *Mumbai Mirror* and other such fine newspapers, said Shamoo with a smile, and maybe they will make a movie about us later.

Oh yes, said Bhatkoo, this plan of arrest and jail is the other reason why Netaji told us to keep this part of the plan secret from you both.

Yes, said Shamoo, he thought you might not be agreeable.

Just then I felt some motion that was different from the regular rocking of the gentle Arabian Seas. After wondering for one minute about it, I realized the cause as I saw the lights of Haji Ali move farther away from us. The cause of the feeling of motion was the actual physical motion of the onion boat on which we were stationed. I looked at Yoosuf, who had stepped up to the wheelhouse and was operating the radar or some other marine object.

Feel free to sleep for some time, he said, I will wake you when we arrive in Pakistan.

28

At first, all of us Indians voiced protest and made threats of suicide and murder and other terrible things, but since we had no weapons and these Pakistanis at least had some mutton-choppers and one unloaded AK47, most of the threats were useless as devices of negotiation. But then, after we got tired of shouting and begging and crying, I thought about the situation and realized that perhaps it was not so bad. Probably sailing to Pakistan is a better short-term plan than appearing in *Mumbai Mirror* in my black kurta-pajama and being implicated in either terrorism or onion-theft, both of which carried penalty of death.

Of course, my sweet wife would be quite angry in both cases, but at least if I telephone her from Pakistan she cannot give me any physical beating. If I am interred at Arthur

Road Jail in Mumbai, then the wife can definitely come to visit me and beat me quite badly inside the jail, where beatings from wives are tolerated for thirty minutes per day.

I was not sure how the visa situation would work out in Pakistani territory, but since I was not carrying my passport, there would be no place to stamp the visa anyway, so it was pointless to worry about it. And so finally I just took Yoosuf's advice and lay down and put my head on a bag of onions and went to sleep for the night.

I awoke some hours later due to massive commotion and the sounds of some kind of loud engines and what-not. I climbed up outside of the onion-hatch, but immediately I had to shield my eyes from the massive winds that blew in my face. When I managed to make my eyes into tiny slits so I could see the cause of the winds, I was surprised to see a massive helicopter with protruding weaponry sitting on the deck of the large onion-ship. Some men and women in uniforms were standing on the deck near the helicopter, and they obviously had command of the situation due to their advanced weaponry and fashionable military-type uniforms.

At first I thought the Chinese had found us, but these people did not look like the Chinese gymnasts that win gold medals at the Olympics, and they were definitely not Indians, so I was not sure what to think. It appeared that Yoosuf and Iqbal were engaged in very serious conversations with them, and I watched as two of the military-type women came towards me and just smiled little bit and then went to the onion-hatch as if to check for something.

One of the women came back up and shouted something

in a language that was not Hindi and not Urdu and not English. It may have been Chinese, because I do not know Chinese, but since these people did not look like Chinese, I guessed that it was not Chinese. It did not matter, I thought, because with all that weaponry and what-not, it was obvious that they were there to kill us.

As I prepared once more to die, the military-type people said some other things to Yoosuf and Iqbal, and then they simply got back into their helicopter and increased the speed of the rotors, which lifted the helicopter up. They flew away after that, and I was left there in confusion.

Israelis, said Iqbal to me.

Israelis, said Yoosuf.

What, I said as I wondered if Netaji had made a quadruple deal. After all, Israel is also a great ally of India, and we are always doing some kind of business with them.

Yes, said Iqbal, they had apparently heard about Netaji's plan to sell weapons to the Indian government, and they wanted to intercept the gun-boats and sink them.

And so, said Yoosuf, when we told them how the gun-boats were already sunk, they were quite happy and they flew off.

But why do they want the guns to be sunk, I said.

Because Israel has just moved to the number one ranking as a supplier of arms and ammunition to India, said Iqbal, and so they do not want any side deals going on that could cause India to buy less arms from them. It is a simple case of supply and demand.

Now that I had already got a sufficient understanding of supply and demand mechanics, I understood this issue, and so I nodded my head and looked around and smiled when I noticed that the sun was slowly coming up over the horizon. As I enjoyed the slow breeze and increasing warmth, another brainwave hit me.

You said that Israel has only just recently become number one arms supplier to India, I said, and so which country was the previous number one supplier?

Iqbal said some answer, but I could not hear it, because from off to the side of our boat came a massive sound of waves and more commotion of engines and what-not, and a large black metallic object rose up out of the sea like a black python made of metal. Only when the full thing was above the water surface did I recognize it to be a submarine, and then when I saw the famous-looking red and white and blue flag painted on the side next to the letters USA, I realized which country was recently overtaken by Israel as India's number one arms supplier.

29

The Americans I think wanted the same thing as the Israelis, but at least I could understand their speech. The big boss man had a very loud and clear voice, and those of us that knew English had no problems with hearing him. He and his men boarded our ship, but he did not point any guns at us. At first I wondered why that was the case. After all, if they think we have five thousand kilos of guns and bombs with us, then at least they would show some force to terrorize us into handing over said weapons. But soon I understood why they were so casual.

We've been watching you guys, said the big boss American man, and it don't seem like you have what we're looking for.

You are looking for the thousands of kilos of guns and bombs that is to be delivered to the Indian government, I said in a loud voice that I hoped would prove that I was the big boss Indian man on our onion-boats.

Yeah, said the boss man, and you guys sure don't have it.

No, I said, surely not.

What did you tell the Israelis? he asked.

The truth, I said, which is what we tell everyone on account of us being Gandhians.

Ah yes Gandhi, he said with a smile, that tiny guy did a lot of major shit.

Yes, I said, major.

Kicked the goddamn Brits out of your country didn't he, said the American.

Oh yes, I said, kicked them with extreme prejudice but nonviolently of course.

The American seemed to find this funny, and he looked at a few of his soldiers and they all laughed. I noticed that some of his soldiers were women also, and I wondered at the wondrousness of the American and Israeli militaries that they have so many women stationed in foreign countries. Of course, our Indian forces have women as well, but not so many yet I think. Most of our deadliest women are still in the homes beating up their husbands and other enemies. At this I laughed in order to hide my sadness and fear at my wife's reaction when I telephone her from Pakistan. Perhaps she will leave me, I thought, and join the military and go to some far-off place to inflict damage on the enemies of India.

What's with all these goddamn onions man, shouted one of the American soldiers who had been sent to the cargo hatches to verify that there were indeed no guns or bombs on board.

I explained the situation to the American boss man, and he simply shook his head and I think he was not sure whether to laugh or cry, and I wondered if he was missing his wife as well or if she was with him in the foreign lands and seas that he was stationed in. I was feeling quite friendly suddenly, and so I asked him precisely this question.

That's classified information little buddy, he said with some seriousness but not real seriousness because behind him some of his soldiers laughed.

Oh she is on a secret mission is it, I asked with great excitement.

Don't ask don't tell, said one of the soldiers.

Hell yeah baby, said another soldier who hit the other soldier on the palm like how those basketball players do it and now even our cricket players are doing it.

Remember yourself soldier, said the boss man and this time he was serious and his men and women kept quiet and stood at attention.

With the laughter and the jokes finished, and also the onion inspection complete, it seemed like the Americans had no more use for our time. And so they went back into their big black submarine, and the big metal thing smoothly went back under the Arabian Seas, and things were calm and quiet again like all these were normal and unsurprising events on the high seas. I was still little bit sleepy, but I thought I might as well stay awake because, based on the trajectory of events, I thought it was obvious that some other nation's air or sea vehicle would appear suddenly and ask us questions or make jokes or maybe simply kill us.

At least no one is actually after the onions, said Veeru with relief.

Yes, said Yoosuf, and soon we will be out of Indian waterspace and heading for Pakistani waterspace.

And just then, as per my prediction, we heard a loud horn. When we turned in the direction of the horn, we saw a massive ship that was flying the beautiful tricolor flag of the Indian nation. I immediately thought to salute and sing the National Anthem, but then I thought perhaps the Pakistanis would be offended, and so I just stood up and faced the flag and sang the National Anthem in my mind.

My mental singing was soon interrupted by some commotion behind me. Yoosuf and Veeru were frantically looking at some charts and some instruments like GPS or GSM or GQ, and Iqbal was just standing there and holding the steering wheel of the ship as if in expectation of some instructions to turn. The instructions came, and Iqbal turned, and then suddenly Yoosuf shouted something to Veeru, and Veeru shouted something to the henchman on the other onion boat, and they immediately switched off the boat engines and dropped the anchors into the waters.

At this I was surprised. I expected that perhaps we will try to escape by leaving Indian waterspace and entering Pakistani waterspace or something like that, and so I asked Yoosuf.

No, he said, Pakistani waterspace could be even more dangerous than Indian waterspace.

And so, said Veeru, we have affixed ourselves in the small part of the waterspace that is classified as international waterspace.

Iqbal smiled at me as if he agreed that this was a good idea, and so I eased my mind and finished the National Anthem by singing the last few lines out loud.

By then, as if timed to the end of my National Anthem recital, the big Indian Navy boat was close enough for someone in a white uniform to shout at us through one of those cone-shaped devices that magnifies the shouting and makes it sound like an Indian robot is shouting at you.

This is the Indian Navy, said the Indian robot.

Okay, I shouted back in my normal shouting voice.

You will hand over the weapons cargo, said the Indian robot.

No weapons, I shouted, only onions.

At hearing this, the robot put down his cone-machine and started to talk to some other man in a white uniform but with a different hat. Soon the robot-voice came back to face us and shouted once more.

You will hand over the onions cargo, said the Indian robot.

Come and take it then, shouted Yoosuf before I could say anything.

I was surprised that Yoosuf, the man who was prepared to fight the Chinese warlords with nothing but some mutton-choppers, would simply hand over the onions to the Indian government.

The robot-shouter did some more covert conversing with his captain, and from the looks of it, the captain was making some kind of fuss and pointing at an imaginary line in the water. Soon the robot-voice came back to us and shouted again.

Come closer, he shouted.

No, said Yoosuf with a smile, you come and take the onions if you want it.

See, said Veeru to me, they know they cannot board our vessel because we are in international waters and they do not have jurisdiction here.

I stared at Veeru and I must say I had a great respect for his understanding of international maritime law. These Pakistanis were not so stupid as the Indian newspapers say, and I felt proud to be associated with such smart men.

Yoosuf smiled at me and patted me on the shoulder.

You should be proud of your government, he said, because they are good and observant about such global rules.

Yes, said Veeru, because since no one is looking they could just come on board and squash us like how I have squashed those Pakistani mountain rats when they steal a chicken kabaab from my kabaab-grill.

Yes, I said with pride, the Indian government is efficient and smooth and honest and wondrous.

Iqbal made a sound that appeared to be one of mockery, but I ignored it. Then some more sounds of mockery came, and I could see that even Yoosuf and Veeru were laughing at my unbiased display of love and respect for my great government.

Let us not get carried away, said Yoosuf, and instead focus on the task at hand.

Yes, said Iqbal, because these Navy buggers will not break the rules, but they may bend them by forcing us to move over into Indian waters, and then they will board us with extreme prejudice.

Ay, shouted the Navy bugger, come on over here now you stupid buggers. You cannot refuse a direct order from the Indian Navy.

No, shouted Veeru, you come here.

And this went on for some time until the sun moved

higher in the sky and everyone went back inside their shaded accommodations areas for some refreshments and maybe some gargling with salt water to re-energize the vocal cords for more shouting between international waterspace and Indian waterspace. As we sat inside the onion-boat's one large room, I was quite happy with the situation, but it seemed that Yoosuf and Iqbal, the two answer-men, were not so pleased with this political stalemate that we had engineered through the smartness of these Pakistanis.

The problem, said Iqbal, is they will have more supplies and hence can simply wait for us to run out of food and water.

And then, said Yoosuf, we will be forced to appeal to them to save us from starvation.

The thought of starvation at first made me hungry, but then I received a massive brainwave.

No, I said, we will win because we are Gandhians.

Iqbal looked at me like I had swallowed some salt water and gone mad, and then I think he understood.

Hunger strike, said Iqbal with a smile.

Hunger strike, I said.

And now our Gandhian adventures had truly reached Himalayan proportions.

30

Of course, the key thing about a hunger strike is that the opposing party must be made aware that you are on a hunger strike. If they do not know, then chances are you will simply die without anyone realizing until you are dead. And so we had to do something very brave and perhaps foolish, but necessary.

We stood on the deck of our boat, and in plain sight of the Indian Navy people, we emptied all our remaining food items into the sea. Then I shouted to them and explained that we are Gandhians and we would be on a hunger strike up until death or the time when the Navy ship retreats and disappears from sight. If death comes first, I told them, then it will be due to the persistent pursuit of the Indian Navy, and since the deaths would occur in international waterspace, it would no doubt result in a massive international war.

At first the Navy sailors laughed at us, but then their captain came out and listened to the situation, and all the Navy people went serious. They attempted to speak to us some more, but we refused any reply in order to conserve energy for our hunger strike. I was not well experienced in hunger, but from my limited understanding of biological warfare, I knew that in absence of regular food, the human body would simply begin to digest itself beginning with non-vital organs like ear-lobe and spleen.

The Pakistanis had been very quiet since the initiation of this plan, and I was not sure if they were upset about following a Gandhian rule or if they were also simply conserving energy. Of course, we secured all persons' agreement before throwing away the food. And we were not so stupid, because we did not throw away the fresh drinking water. We knew that proper hunger strike rules allow for drinkage of water on a daily basis.

But of course, our master plan was quite simple, and in fact our entire hunger strike strategy was dependent on this master plan. Since death was not part of our plan, we would still have to survive long enough to arrive at Pakistani shores where we could buy fresh biryani or kabaabs. And since we were in the company of two great Pakistani preparers of food and one great Indian consumer of food, we knew the great secret of the onion.

Yes. The secret is that one can survive on onion alone indefinitely. And by indefinitely, I mean full life and even beyond if necessary. The onion has very high vitamin and mineral content, as well as all major food groups such as spice and flavor. So we knew that once we have defeated the Indian Navy, we could survive on onions until we reached the kabaab-grills of the Pakistani mainland.

The Indian Navy did not give up immediately. But sometime during the nighttime, when I awoke to make sure my ear-lobes had not been digested by my starving body, I saw that the Indian Navy ship had lifted its anchors and was preparing to leave. In great joy I woke up everyone on our onion boats.

We have won, I shouted, through Gandhian tactics!

All the remaining Indians and Pakistanis crawled out of their sleeping holes and joined me on deck to take delight in our victory over the Indian Navy, and once the big ship had turned and moved far from us, we celebrated by opening one bag of onions and sharing some sweet and spicy slices in the clear night as we bounced gently in the international waterspace that lies between the seas owned by Pakistan and India.

We have won for now, said Yoosuf as his eyes watered from victory emotions and onion juices, but we still have a long journey left and who knows what is to come.

31

Luckily no one knew beforehand what was to come, or else we might have surrendered our onions immediately and taken refuge in the Indian Navy ship.

The storm came very silently, but when it arrived, things became quite noisy. The boats were thrown about like little buckets, and if there had not been a thick rope connecting our two onion boats, we would have been separated forever. The rains were quite heavy, and combined with the waves it resulted in a very wet experience for all of us. At one point the movement of the boats became so extreme that we had to all go down to the lowest onion hatch and jam ourselves between the bags of onions so that our heads did not get bashed against the wooden sides of the boat.

This may have continued all day and all night. I could not

tell because the sky was dark from dark clouds, and being in the onion hatch for so long made us lose sense of time as well as sense of balance. Even the calm answer-men Yoosuf and Iqbal were shouting in fear as the boat seemed sure to turn upside down and convert us into floating objects never to be found again.

Then we heard and felt a loud crash, and our boat became still.

At first I thought the storm had suddenly stopped, but I could hear the rain still coming down from above our heads and the thunder making thundering noises. Then I thought that maybe we have been taken upon the back of the giant turtle that lives in the water, but I knew that the turtle was just a mythological story, and anyway it lives in the Bay of Bengal, which is on the other side of India. Regardless, for at least two-three hours more no one was feeling balanced enough to go upstairs and check. But then, since we had not been moving for a long time, and also the rain pressure seemed to have lowered slightly, I took on the heroic job of going upstairs to encounter the giant Bengali turtle or whatever other danger that was in our path.

When I reached upstairs I found that the sky was looking lighter and the wind was slower. But more interesting was that it seemed there was no turtle or anything, and in fact we had hit upon some land area, because I could see in the not-so-far distance some sandy beaches and even some lights beyond the beaches. I thanked the gods for securing our safety, because some time back there had been no hope of our survival. Even our remaining drinking water had been spilled, and although the rainwater is drinkable, we had not concerned ourselves with capturing any of it.

I quickly told the rest of the people that we are saved and perhaps we are even in Pakistan now. Yoosuf and Iqbal and Veeru came up quickly, and then the other Pakistani from the other boat showed his face and waved to us to indicate that he was alive. Bhatkoo and Shamoo were also fine, but they had been very quiet for the past two days, ever since their betrayal had been exposed and I had threatened to chop up Shamoo and his non-vitals.

Yoosuf went to check the GPS or GQ-meter, but apparently the water had destroyed it. Same thing with our cell phones, which had been bashed and drenched along with our bodies.

I hope we are in Pakistan, he said, but I cannot be sure.

We will have to go find some people on the shore and ask them, I said.

Then I worried about my visa situation. If this was Pakistan, then would they not arrest me immediately for being an alien lander? But then I remembered that Pakistani and Indian people are basically the same, so I would just say I am a Pakistani and give some verbal abuses to India and then ask for some mutton biryani so that my starving body does not digest itself.

I will come with you, said Yoosuf.

I will come too, said Iqbal.

Me also, said Veeru.

No, said Yoosuf to Veeru, you stay here and protect the onions. Besides, if we are arrested or killed, you can then immediately push the boats out to sea and complete our mission.

Yes okay, said Veeru.

I looked at Iqbal, and he looked very tired and weak, and so I told him to stay behind in case this is Pakistan and I am taken away to be fed to the mountain rats. This way he can telephone my wife and tell her that I died in a Gandhian manner at least.

And so Yoosuf and myself stepped out of the boat into the waist-high water and began to make our way towards the smooth pebbles and sand of the shore. There was no one to be seen, but it was either early in the morning or late in the evening, neither of which is a popular time for beach parties. The walk out of the beach and towards the lights was longer than expected, but at least it was good that we had been deposited on a beach that was within a village. Finally we arrived at one establishment that looked like a restaurant, but a very cheap and empty place. There was no signpost on it, and therefore we could not see if the language here was Hindi or Urdu. So now we still did not know if this was India or Pakistan, but at this point it did not matter as long as we were given some food and water.

The restaurant owner came out to us and I spoke to him in Hindi and Yoosuf spoke to him in Urdu, and he replied to us in some mixture of Hindi and Urdu, which is not helpful for determining location, because Hindi and Urdu are approximately same-sounding in words and grammar and what-not. And so we just asked him what place this was.

Porbandar, he said.

At this I was taken aback, and I started to believe that perhaps our Gandhian adventures were not over and perhaps the Gandhian adventures had actually just begun.

I looked at Yoosuf and smiled. It appeared that Yoosuf was not familiar with the village of Porbandar, and so I informed him with pride.

Porbandar is in the Indian state of Gujarat, I said.

Ah Gujarat, said Yoosuf, that is not bad because Gujarat is a border state to Pakistan. But Porbandar I have not heard of.

Porbandar, I said with Gandhian calmness, is the birthplace of our man Bapu. Gandhiji was born here on this very soil.

32

Once we returned to the boats and informed the others of our symbolic landing place, everyone was quiet for some time, and I think I understood finally why sailors and such people are so superstitious when they are saved from deathly storms and other sea emergencies. Of course, for us it was even more reason to be superstitious due to the fact that our Gandhian pursuits had resulted in our being deposited on the beach where young Bapu must have played as a child. Gandhi of course must have been a nonviolent child, I thought, but nonetheless he would have been civilly disobedient and possibly a handful for his parents.

Of course, Gujarati people are known as great businesspeople in India, and since as it is Porbandar is a poor village, the restaurant owner was not impressed with our Gandhian credentials since the credentials were unaccompanied by any money whatsoever. The owner gave us some fresh water and also some bread and lentils so we would not die on his property, but he did not let us use his cell phone or order any of the fancy dishes on his menu.

We have onions, said Bhatkoo suddenly from the rear of our group.

How many, said the restaurant owner.

Lots, said Shamoo, and lots.

Bring them, said the restaurant owner, and I will allow you to use my cell phone and also I will prepare some fine baingan bharta and fresh rotis for everyone.

Baingan bharta is an eggplant dish that is very delicious, and roti is of course the wheat flat bread that everywhere is eaten but just now sounded like the best dish of all. I turned to Shamoo and Bhatkoo and smiled at them for the first time since my unrestrained slapping of their faces, and when I saw their faces light up due to my smile, I felt that maybe I had been unnecessarily harsh with them. After all, they were poor servants who had stayed in my home and suspended themselves from my ceiling. They were only acting on orders from their master Netaji, and although the double and triple deals were very complicated and somewhat suspicious, in general even Netaji's intentions seemed okay.

As Bhatkoo and Shamoo returned to the boats to fetch a five-kilo bag of onions, we discussed our plan of action.

We must telephone our people in Pakistan, said Veeru, and have them send jeeps or trucks to the border.

At this point no one wanted to get back into the boats due

to previous sea emergencies, and plus we had observed that the propellers and rudder of the big boat had been broken off in the storm. Yoosuf and Veeru wanted to use some onions to perhaps arrange for a truck or bullock carts to carry them and the remaining onions to the border where they would meet some other Pakistanis and complete their journey.

And we must telephone Netaji, said Iqbal, and shout at him for his multiple dealings that almost got us killed.

Yes, I said, but first at least let us tell him to arrange for some train tickets or bus tickets for us so we can return to Mumbai. And then we will talk with him about these dealings when we are safely home.

Iqbal smiled and nodded and I think he was impressed at how calm and focused I had become since my dealings with the Americans and the Indian Navy and now the Gujarati businessmen.

Bhatkoo and Shamoo returned with the onion bag, and judging by the reaction of the restaurant owner, we had priced the onions very low. He gave us his cellphone to keep, and he even opened some cold drinks for us to have with the bharta and roti. Yoosuf made his calls to the Pakistanis first, and then he gave us the phone to call Netaji and others in Mumbai.

Netaji must have been waiting for the call because he answered immediately and with great concern in his voice.

You are all safe, he said with relief, even Bhatkoo and Shamoo.

Yes, I said, but the weapons and the onions are all gone.

No matter, he said, no matter at all.

His lack of concern for the goods and major concern for

our persons made even Iqbal calm down, and we made arrangements for him to use electronic and long-distance payment methods to secure tickets for all four of us on the train to Mumbai.

Come quickly, he said to me as I was about to put down the phone, because your wife has found me and I am being abused in manners that is even worse than when the Japanese arrested me for public urination in 1973.

33

How my wife must have found Netaji I do not know, but this way at least she would unleash some anger and beatings upon that man first, which would hopefully reduce my own quota of beatings. And also I was happy that at least Netaji could inform her of my safety, and I would not need to call her just now. I was too weak and full of eggplant and roti to endure even verbal abuse just now, and I happily sat in the restaurant and took a nap as the Pakistanis along with Iqbal and Bhatkoo and Shamoo went out to the town to find some place to sleep for the night.

Bhatkoo and Shamoo returned to fetch me in a few hours, and we all went to a small Gujarati guest house owned by a very sweet old man and woman. These owners did not ask us many questions, and the little bit of money we had asked from the restaurant owner as part of the onion exchange was sufficient for three big sleeping rooms and with inclusive dinner and then breakfast the next morning.

Iqbal had gone with the Pakistanis to ask about some lorries or bullock carts to transport the onions. I did not worry about it because Iqbal is a good negotiator, and I felt it would be quite easy for him to arrange for someone to drive the Pakistanis to the border in exchange for one or two bags of onions.

I laughed at how funny it was that the onion problem was actually to our benefit now because the shortage had made our bags very useful as currency after our sea emergency. Of course, at that point, perhaps because we were in Bapu's hometown, I did not think this would cause any problems. So when Iqbal came running into our guest room covered with dirt and sweat from running, I was shocked.

They have been taken, he shouted.

Who has been taken, I shouted.

The onions, he shouted, and the Pakistanis.

Means what, I said in terror.

Means we found some people who said they will drive trucks with our supplies, said Iqbal, and when they found out we would pay them in onions, they were fine with it.

And then? I asked.

And then we took them back to where the boats were tied up and began to load the onions, said Iqbal, and once the onions were loaded they grabbed hold of us and laughed and said they are seizing all the onions.

How did you run away? I asked.

With my feet you silly bugger, shouted Iqbal. How does it matter?

My brother in life appeared almost mad with anger and worry, and I too was worried about what would happen to our Pakistani brothers at the hands of some onion-crazed Gujarati mob. Death could easily result from mobbing activities, and especially if mobbing is being done against Pakistanis. In Gujarat there has been lots of anti-Muslim propaganda over the past few years, and sometimes these poor villagers who do not have schooling and do not have any Pakistani friends may react with extremist tendencies.

We must save them, I shouted, Bhatkoo-Shamoo come here you two.

Bhatkoo and Shamoo were in the next room, and they came running when I called. I explained the situation while Iqbal washed his face and did some actions which I think were Muslim prayer techniques that I had never seen him use previously.

Quickly we hurried away, but at that point we had no plan for rescue. In fact, we did not even know where to go in search of our Pakistani brothers, but now Bhatkoo and Shamoo came to the forefront and we were glad to have them with us.

Shamoo will use his tracking mechanism, said Bhatkoo, so let us first go to the sea shore where the abduction of onions and Pakistanis occurred.

I wondered if Shamoo had affixed yet another tracking device to the onion bags or something, but it was nothing to do with electronics or any such artificial mechanisms.

I was once a tracker of tigers in West Bengal, he said proudly.

You used to hunt tigers? I asked in surprise.

No of course not, he said in anger, Bengal tiger is not for hunting but for appreciation only.

Yes of course, I said, that is why I asked.

Anyway, said Shamoo, I used to work for Bengal Tourism Board and do tracking for tours and such things.

I see, said Iqbal, and so you will track these monkeys that have stolen our Pakistanis and the onions.

Yes no problem, said Shamoo, I will do it with great precision.

We got to the sea shore and noted that the boats had been cleaned out of onions and there was no sign of anything at that place. Shamoo immediately began to look for the truck tracks in the ground, and they were quite easily visible due to the wet sand of the beach. In fact even I could have done the tracking based on those muddy tire tracks.

No, said Bhatkoo, the real tracking magic will be shown once the tracks are on the road and the mud has dried and fallen off.

Now I saw his point, and as we followed the mud tracks, soon they disappeared from sight, and once we got to an intersection in the road, I was lost for which way to go.

This way, said Shamoo with confidence.

How do you know? I questioned.

Shamoo appeared to be offended by my questioning. Still, he had betrayed us before, and now I did not want to worry about hurting feelings when the lives of our new brothers were at risk.

Sir, said Shamoo, I would not betray again.

I know, I said, and so let us go the way you said.

We started to run down the road, and soon I was tired and thirsty. Even though it was becoming evening time, it was still hot, and the sweat was making me feel very uncomfortable and sticky.

You stay here, said Bhatkoo, and me and Shamoo and Iqbal will run fast.

I did not argue because my feelings were not important when the lives of our Pakistani brothers were at stake. Of course I am not as fit as these skinny men, and so I am not as capable of chasing trucks down the road in the sun. I sat down on a piece of a dead tree near the road and contemplated the situation of how we had been victims of Gandhi's own Gujarati people, but then I remembered that Gandhiji himself would have been upset at my lack of understanding. These are just poor people, and the sight of so many onions which are now so rare and expensive is enough to make anyone do silly things. After all, not everyone can be a Gandhian. It takes time and practice and self-discipline.

As I contemplated all this, the sound of engines became known. I looked to see two trucks driving towards me. They were coming from the same direction that Shamoo and Bhatkoo and Iqbal had run off in, and I expected that either Shamoo and Bhatkoo and Iqbal had been themselves captured, or the trucks had passed them and now my three friends were chasing the trucks still.

I had to think fast, and I did so as per situation requirements. By now I had faced imagined death at the hands of so many different militaries and gods that I was not concerned about it. My job was to stop the trucks, and so I did so by using the god-given advantage of my bulbous body.

I lay down on the road in the direct pathway of the trucks. As Gandhiji had said, I put my faith in the belief that these people, although they may have robbed the onions, are still not bad and so will not simply run over a fallen man. They will stop and check me, or at least they will move me off to the side of the road. This little delay might be enough time for all of us to gather and somehow save the situation.

I closed my eyes as I felt the ground vibrate from the onion-filled trucks. At first the rumbles were so loud that I was certain that I had been wrong and they would simply run my bulbous body over, but at the last minute the first truck stopped, and this forced the second truck to stop.

The driver got out and looked at me but did not approach.

Hello, he said.

I did not budge.

Are you alive, he said.

I did not answer.

Then the driver from the second truck came up and started yelling at the driver of the first truck.

Are you mad or what, he said, why did you brake so suddenly?

The first driver pointed at my bulbous body, and the second driver made a sound of shock and dismay, and I realized that these people might be robbers but are not yet murderers.

Let us load him into the truck and drop him at the hospital, said the second driver.

Okay come, said the first driver.

They both came up and one driver grabbed my hands and the other driver grabbed my legs. I remained still with my eyes closed, and I must say my acting job was first class. They tried to lift me up, but now the beauty of my bulbousness came into effect. Of course the two of them could barely even drag me, and they certainly could not lift me up and put me into the truck. And so they shouted to their friends who were still in the truck.

But who will watch these buggers, one of the friends shouted back.

Yes, said another friend, what if they escape and tell the police we have stolen their onions?

They are tied up, shouted the driver, and so they will be okay for five minutes alone.

Fine, said the friend, we are coming.

Then I felt many hands take hold of me in different parts of my body, and soon I was being lifted up and carried. These robbers were complaining about my weight, and I had never been so happy about my bulbousness. It took at least ten or fifteen minutes before they carried me to the truck and managed to dump me into the cargo area with the onions. As I dropped into the truck, I heard one of the robbers shout.

Ay they are gone, he shouted, those buggers have somehow been untied and have disappeared.

How can that be, shouted the driver, the knots must have been loose.

Impossible, shouted the friend, someone must have rescued them.

There was some more commotion as the robbers ran

around a little bit as if to see if Yoosuf and Veeru and the other Pakistani were hiding, but I do not think they found them. I felt happy and heroic because I knew that Bhatkoo and Shamoo and Iqbal must have come from behind and untied the Pakistanis. And so in the end it was my plan and action that saved the Pakistanis from certain death here in the homeground of Gandhiji.

Of course, now the only problem was that I myself had been caught by these robber buggers.

34

At first I thought maybe my acting job is so good that they will simply deposit me at the hospital and not realize that it was my brainwave that enabled the rescue. But this was not the case, as I found out when two of the robbers got into the truck with me and slapped me to wake me up. I tried to ignore the slaps, but it is hard to be quiet when your face is being slapped.

And so I jumped up and tried to dive from the truck.

This was the mistake, I think. Perhaps if I had simply opened my eyes and tried to pretend to be hurt they may have believed me, but my instinctive attempt to escape proved beyond a doubt that I was the mastermind behind the escape plan.

Ay fatso, said one of the robbers, where will you run to?

Yes, laughed the other robber, your friends have left you and run off.

Now what will you do fatso, laughed the first robber.

And then they started slapping me again, and when I tried to cover my face with my hands, they slapped my hands so hard that my own hands began to hit my face and so it was like I was slapping myself, which is a double insult. So finally I put my hands down and let them slap away. Now I was a true Gandhian, and it hurt a lot.

Eventually the truck began to move quite fast on the bumpy road and the men stopped slapping me so they could hold on to the sides and keep balance. I was not sure where they were taking me, but that was not really my concern. I was still thinking about how I had saved my friends, and for some reason at that point it seemed that if I die now I will be remembered as a martyr as well as an escape mastermind.

But then some thoughts of reality and the prospect of my death resurfaced when the truck stopped. By now it was night, and I was not sure how Shamoo would be able to follow the truck tracks in the dark. And besides, how much could those poor skinny friends of mine be expected to run in one day? Plus, we had been driving on the roads for quite some time now, and even if Shamoo was able to follow, it would take them a long time to reach me due to discrepancy between speed of foot and speed of truck.

The robbers told me to get out of the truck and I did so. We were in some kind of big garage or godown, and by godown I mean warehouse. There were some other trucks in this place, but no other people. I examined my kidnappers and was surprised to see that they were quite young. In fact, they appeared extremely young, younger than my oldest son who is just finishing college at age twenty-one.

You children have no shame, I shouted, to be kidnapping and torturing an old man like me?

Ay shut up you fat old man, shouted one of the boys, or we will continue the slapping and now we will not stop.

At this threat I shut up, but I was staring at each of them intently in the hope of making them feel like a father-type figure is scolding them. But again this was a mistake, because I think they must have not liked their fathers. One of them came up to me with a stick, and now I became very worried for my safety. Slapping is one thing, but to be hit by a stick is quite different. I stood there in preparation, hoping that I would be able to move my head away so that my other body parts could absorb the blow, but just as he was about to strike, another boy shouted.

Stop it Kailash, the boy said, he is already hurt and is not any danger to us now.

The boy Kailash put down his stick immediately, and I looked at the boy who had spoken. He must be the leader, I thought, and so I must try and deal directly with him to secure my freedom.

Thank you young fellow, I said to him.

Shut up, said the leader fellow, or I will let him hit you next time.

Sorry, I said quietly and just sat down in a corner.

The boys all gathered and looked at the onion loads, and I noticed that the load seemed much less than what we had on the boats. I wondered if they had hidden some of the onions at another location, but in listening to their conversation I realized that they had already sold some of them.

What to do with the rest of these, said Kailash.

When nobody answered, he turned to the leader and asked again.

Ay Nitin-bhai, said Kailash, answer me, no?

Quiet, said Nitin, I am thinking.

But Kailash did not seem to want to stay quiet.

There is no one else in Porbandar with capacity to buy so many onions now, said Kailash, and so what to do then? The onions will spoil here and all our trouble will be for nothing.

Of course, I knew that onions take very long to spoil, but I did not want to say this. Better if these robbers become desperate and so try to go out again to sell the onions and perhaps give me a chance for escape.

Onions will not go bad so quickly, said Nitin, and so we can hide them here for many days and even weeks if necessary.

But that will increase the chances of police finding us with stolen goods, said Kailash, and if my father finds out I am arrested he will beat me very badly.

And I will beat you myself if you don't shut up, said Nitin.

This went on for some time and soon I tuned out and began to search for brainwaves in my bulbous head. But the day's action seemed to have drained my intelligence, and I suddenly realized that I was very hungry and thirsty.

May I have some water, I asked politely.

Shut up, said Kailash.

But the boy Nitin stood up and came over to me with a tumbler of water and allowed me to drink.

We will give you some food later when we eat, he said to me.

Now that I saw him from close I could tell he was basically an honest boy but possibly just mischievous. And sometimes without proper education and upbringing, mischievous children can easily turn into criminals without realizing it.

This is the first time you have done something illegal, I told him softly so that others could not hear me.

He did not say anything, but I could tell that he was affected by my statement. Just then I felt some energy due to the water ingestion, and so I pushed forward with the conversation.

Will you kill me, I said.

At this statement the boy jerked his head as if in shock, and I knew that if I pushed him some more, he will feel very guilty and perhaps let me go. But since my instincts were feeling at peak level just then, I sensed it was best not to push too much in front of that Kailash boy. Sometimes when boys are with their friends they feel the need to act tough, and if Nitin shows some weakness in front of his cronies, then perhaps things will get out of hand. I had seen this dynamic many times with my own son, and so I let things be for the time being and just sat back quietly. Nitin went back to the other boys, but I could tell he was thinking about what to do with me, and I knew he was worried. Stealing onions is one thing, but stealing human beings is a different level of crime entirely.

What if those people who escaped go to the police, asked Kailash.

They will not, said Nitin, because I think they spoke in

Urdu and since they wanted to hire the trucks to take them near the border, I think they are Pakistanis.

Oh, said Kailash, I never thought of that. They must be terrorists.

Not all Pakistanis are terrorists, said Nitin.

Correct, said Kailash, but all Pakistanis that come to India are terrorists.

At this all the boys laughed, and even though the joke was a bad joke, it provided some break in the atmosphere. Soon they brought out some food to eat, and once they had finished, Nitin came up to me with some leftover food and one more tumbler of water. But this time he did not stay next to me long enough for me to say anything, and so I ate in silence.

The boys seemed to be doing some secretive talking away from me. I tried to make out what they were saying, but they were speaking too softly. Still, I could tell that Kailash was very angry, and Nitin was trying to explain something to him. After some more argument, Kailash got up and walked off as if in anger. And then Nitin came back to me.

Finish your food, he said, and then I will take you and drop you back in the village.

I did not say anything, because what is the purpose of questioning a plan that benefits me perfectly? But as I finished my food, I found myself questioning the plan after all. Since I was sure that Bhatkoo and Iqbal and Yoosuf and the others would be searching for me, I worried about what would happen if they arrived at the warehouse before I found them in the village. If Nitin is not back here by then and the Kailash boy is in charge, then things could easily get violent.

And not only did I fear for my friends, but actually I also feared for these young boys. After all, I knew that Yoosuf and Veeru had talked about having mutton-choppers, and if provoked, who knows what could happen?

And so I made one more foolish but brave decision.

I will not leave without my onions, I told Nitin when he returned to take my food plate away.

Are you mad, said Nitin, you know that my friend Kailash wants to hit you on the head and throw you into the sea to drown?

If that is what you all end up doing with me then let it be so, I said, but I am not leaving without my onions.

Now this Nitin boy looked truly worried, and I almost felt sorry for him, but then I remembered that this situation was caused by him and his friends, and so let him get worried and scared a little. It will teach him a lesson.

And also, I said, starting from now I am on a hunger strike.

35

I am not sure what Nitin told his friends, but there was not much commotion from that side of the room. I suppose Nitin could have simply tied me up and taken me to the village and thrown me somewhere, and actually I wondered why he did not. My guess was that all the other boys had opposed his idea of releasing me anyway, and so they would not help transport me by force. Soon the boys all went to sleep one by one, but I was alert and ready for action because I knew my own brothers would be arriving at some point to save me.

But of course I was tired and so eventually I fell asleep, and when I awoke it was morning and obviously Iqbal and my Pakistani brothers had not come. As I watched the boys all wake up and give me funny looks, I began to worry that maybe Shamoo had lost the tracks and I was truly on my own. And now I had even given up my chance for freedom, and I did not think Nitin would try and argue with his friends again on my behalf. At this point all I had left was my Gandhian spirit, and so I decided to trust in it.

When they offered me some breakfast, I refused it and repeated loudly that I am on a hunger strike and would starve to death unless they released me along with the remaining batches of my onions. At this most of the boys laughed, and that Kailash bugger came up to me with a dirty smile on his face.

You will not be alive long enough to reach starvation state, he said to me.

You are ready to become a murderer, my son? I asked him loudly.

At this he slapped me hard on the face and laughed.

I am already a murderer, he said, and I will happily become a double-murderer.

This statement scared me, and from what I saw, even some of the other boys got scared a little bit. They all looked at Nitin as if asking him for guidance, but Nitin was quiet and seemed to be purposely ignoring the situation. The room became very quiet, and I began to wish for my friends to come bursting in through the door and wave the mutton-choppers and send these boys running for their lives. But the room stayed quiet, and there was no drama of a rescue attempt, and slowly as the day went on I began to lose hope. As my own hunger built and my desperation grew, I began to even wish for Kailash to kill me so I could end this misery. A hunger strike is not a joke at all, especially when you are hungry like

I was. At least on the boat I had some people to join me in the strike, but here I was alone. Alone and hungry.

One of the boys threw a piece of bread at me, but I let it bounce off my body and sit on the ground. I would not even look at it. Then this suddenly became a game with the boys, and they began to throw more food items at me, and soon there were all kinds of food pieces on the ground around me. Now I was faced with two of the toughest Gandhian tests simultaneously: the test of hunger strike maintenance, and the test of temptation.

At least Kailash seemed to have stopped threatening to kill me, and I could see that even he was laughing with his friends and throwing bread and other things at me. He looked like a boy again and not a murderer, and I began to think that he was lying about being a murderer and certainly lying about intending to kill me. I had seen this dynamic also before with groups of young boys, when one of them tries to act extra tough and dangerous but it is probably due to lack of self-confidence. His father must have been quite mean to him, I thought, and not given him enough encouragement and attention.

And then came my latest brainwave, just as a piece of roti bounced off my nose as if to tell me I had hit upon the perfect plot.

Yes, I thought, I will focus my energies and Gandhian spirit on this Kailash boy.

I laughed internally as I watched Kailash laughing at me. First they laugh at you, then they fight you, then they give up, and then you win.

36

I am ready to die, I told Kailash in a calm and confident voice while staring at him directly but not in a confrontational way.

The boys had finished up their food, and some of them had left, perhaps to go for work or to their homes or something. Nitin and Kailash and one other boy had remained, and they had tied me up after allowing me to go to the bathroom. Only Nitin and Kailash were close to me, and so I took this as a good moment to begin a Gandhian dialogue with this poor boy.

I am ready to die, I said again.

No one can be ready to die, said Kailash with a look of scornfulness.

A Gandhian is always ready to die in the pursuit of truth, I said.

Hah, said Kailash, and what truth are you pursuing?

Whatever it is, I said smugly, it is not your concern.

You are a fatso fool, he said and tried to ignore me.

I am no different from you, I said, because you are also ready to die for your cause, are you not?

What cause? he said absentmindedly.

The cause of robbery and thuggery and quick profit, I said and I gave Nitin a quick look and saw that he flinched.

No one will be dying except for you, said Kailash.

Then what is the delay, I said, I already told you I am ready to die.

At this Kailash was quiet, and I could see now that I was correct. Without the full audience of his boys, he was not as aggressive and angry, and now I felt I was close to the third or fourth stage in the Gandhian progression of passive resistance: soon he would give up, and then I would win.

I wondered if I should explain to him that if he killed me then he was risking his own life either at the ends of some Pakistani mutton-choppers or the hangman's rope, but I decided not to say all this. My feeling was that Nitin and the others must have already understood this, because I had heard all of them mention fear of police before. And so my best plan would be to try and simply get them to release me.

But of course by now I had become married to my cause, the cause of the onions. I knew that one way or the other, the onions had to get back into the hands of Yoosuf and Veeru, and the more nonviolence involved the better. I wondered how to explain to these boys the importance of the onion mission, and how it was a miracle that on our Gandhian mission we landed in Gandhiji's hometown, and how our delivery of the onions to the Pakistanis would in fact contribute in some way to greater peace along the borders that even Gujarat shared with our neighboring country.

Then I remembered how my own son loved to listen to stories even up until he went to college. And so I took one more look at these boys who were sitting quietly after their meal, and I began to tell the story of our Gandhian adventures.

I began at the beginning, and I described everything. I told of the small onion problem that turned into a massive expedition that took us far away from home and onto the high Arabian Seas where we encountered Israelis and Americans and Indians and other sea creatures, and I could see that these boys were captivated and mesmerized by my tales.

And by the time the doors of the warehouse burst open and Iqbal and Bhatkoo and Shamoo came in with big sticks and behind them Yoosuf and Veeru waving mutton-choppers, these three young boys that were not really bad people but just mischievous and unfortunate not to have proper upbringing had already untied me, and we were drinking tea together, and they had already promised to drive the Pakistanis to the border and then even drop me and Iqbal and Bhatkoo and Shamoo to the train station.

After I quieted down my rescuers and explained everything, the situation came again under control, and everyone finally sat down and the boys even got some more tea and water for everyone. It was indeed a Gandhian moment of epic proportions, where those that were once enemies are now drinking tea while sitting on the ground in Gandhiji's hometown in Gujarat.

How far is the border from here? said Yoosuf after some time.

Few hours' drive, said Kailash, but first we will have to go in the other direction.

Why is that, said Yoosuf, to avoid border patrols?

Kailash and Nitin and the other boy laughed as if the concept of border patrols was a funny joke.

No no, said Nitin, we know how to go straight through the border without any worry of patrols.

Then why go in the opposite direction? said Veeru.

Because, said Kailash, first we will go and retrieve the batches of onions that we rudely stole from you and sold off.

37

It turned out that the boys had sold the onions to that same restaurant owner whom we had met first near the sea shore. They must have arranged with him at the sea shore itself, and then they had driven to his storage place far off, which is where I encountered them by laying on the road.

There was no issue with retrieving the onions, because there were ten of us and this poor restaurant man was alone with his wife and one old cow in the field. Nitin and Kailash and the boys were even so good that they returned the money to him, but only after subtracting some amount for the petrol costs, and this was only because that money had already been spent. Still, the restaurant man was very scared and even surprised that we gave back his money. Then immediately both trucks began to drive in the direction of the

Pakistani border, and Yoosuf made one more phone call to his people to say he is coming.

Our journey was very quiet, because I think all of us were little bit sad that our Gandhian adventures were coming to a close. I could tell that Iqbal was feeling as sad as me, and Yoosuf and Veeru I think were quiet because of sadness as well. It is like how when you are enduring a stressful experience it feels stressful and you want it to stop, but when it stops and you are released from the stress you silently wish for that feeling of excitement once more.

We will meet again, I finally said out loud to my Pakistani brothers who were sitting across from us in the back of one of the onion trucks.

Without doubt, said Yoosuf with a smile.

We will consider this business unfinished until you have eaten our specially prepared mutton biryani and chicken kabaabs, said Veeru.

Perhaps we will kidnap you again and make you cook for us, I said with a smile as I rubbed my bulbous stomach which actually had shrunk little bit after two hunger strikes and all that jogging in the hot sun.

You will not need to kidnap us, said Yoosuf, because we would gladly come and cook for you.

It was nightfall when we arrived at the border, and by this time Iqbal pointed out that we had missed our train back to Mumbai. It was not a big concern, because the tickets were transferable and so we would just take the morning train. It was more important to say goodbye to our new Pakistani brothers and our new Gujarati friends.

There was no border patrol to be seen as Nitin and Kailash had promised, and indeed, there was not even a visible border at the point of our crossing. Finally we saw some lights in the distance, and Yoosuf made one more phone call to confirm that it was indeed his Pakistani people. We drove up to them and stopped.

There was much hugging and loud voices of congratulations from the receiving Pakistanis, and they seemed to be peaceful people like Yoosuf and Veeru, and we did not see any guns or anything. Nitin and Kailash and those other boys seemed nervous and suspicious at first, but soon everyone was introduced and everyone realized that we are all basically the same people, and just like there is no visible border where we stand, there is no real difference between us.

Everyone began to transfer the onions from the Indian trucks to the Pakistani trucks, and when the first Pakistani truck was filled and they began to load the second truck, Veeru gave out a shout from the back.

Ay, he said to his people, what are these bags here?

Oh not to worry, said one of his people, that is some fresh goat and chicken meat that we picked up along the way. We will make a camp and cook it later when we are back in the interior of Pakistan.

No, said Yoosuf with a smile, we will cook it now.

A great cheer came up from the other Pakistanis, and I guessed that these people had missed the great cooking skills of Yoosuf and Veeru, and so even I shouted in joy with them. Quickly they unloaded the fresh meat and other cooking supplies, and Bhatkoo and Shamoo and Kailash and Nitin and some of the Pakistanis found some firewood and started up a great fire right there on the invisible border of our two great nations.

One big bag of onions was opened up, and we all took part in the peeling and chopping of the sweet bulbous bulb that had brought all of us to this place. Some others shared with the grinding of spices and dicing of tomatoes and shredding of chillies and boiling of rice for the biryani and mincing of chicken meat for the kabaabs. Everyone's hands had been involved in each of the food dishes, and in that way it was as symbolic as even the way the crescent moon was sitting in the sky and smiling and laughing at us.

Of course, the final mixing of the ingredients and supervision of the cooking was done by the masters, Yoosuf and Veeru, and when it was ready, we all sat together and gave praise to God without calling God by name.

And then we ate.

38

The food of course was as magical as the situation, and if I try to describe it with words even the best words would be an insult to it. Even now as I write this, Iqbal, the skinny one who does not think of food as I do, is reminiscing about that biryani and those kabaabs. But I think both of us know what all great cooks and lovers of food know: that the quality and taste of the food cannot be considered separately from the occasion and circumstances of preparation of that food. And so we will let go of talk of that occasion of the food and the cooking and the celebrations around the fire in the night which must have been just like in the old days before there was any border between India and Pakistan.

Suffice it to say that no adventurous or unfortunate occurrence stood in our pathway that night, and the onions were transferred properly and we ourselves were transported back to Porbandar and to the train station just in time for the morning train back to Mumbai.

Of course, my wife and Iqbal's wife and even Netaji were waiting at the train station. My sweet wife was so happy to see me alive that if she was angry, all the anger was gone or too well hidden for even me to notice. Netaji gave Bhatkoo and Shamoo hugs, which was quite surprising I think to them.

Iqbal and I had beforehand decided that there was no reason to take Netaji to task at the train station itself. We will let Bhatkoo and Shamoo give Netaji the details of the adventures, and we will simply go home with our wives and tell them of our heroism and of how our Gandhian spirit saved us from many imagined deaths.

When we returned to our lane in this greatest city of Mumbai, the pao-bhaji-walla's helper came running up to me and presented me with a free plate of special bhaji with extra bread that was double-buttered. I was surprised, and looked across at the pao-bhaji-walla. From that one look I could tell that he must have been the one who directed my wife to Netaji, and I laughed at myself for not realizing this earlier.

After spending the full day and the next day also with no one but my sweet darling baby wife, I finally picked up the telephone and dialed for Iqbal, my brother in life.

Should we go out for a walk, I asked him.

Yes, he said, in fact I was about to call you for the same thing.

And so we met out on the old familiar street and walked to the end of the lane. The street was the same, but since me and Iqbal were now different, everything in sum was also different. We greeted the pao-bhaji-walla, who had started giving me one free plate of special bhaji every day, and I ate my special bhaji and did some chit-chat about life and love and philosophy and what-not. By now it seemed like through the word of many mouths, the entire community of our lane knew of our adventures, and everyone was interested in our philosophies on life and marriage and all kinds of small things that are not really the business of Gandhians. But of course we cannot disappoint the people, and so we would give our viewpoints with great immediacy and extreme prejudice but also with reminders that Gandhian principles must pervade all of life's pursuits.

After one or two hours of answering questions and giving advices, we decided to walk outside our lane and perhaps go to the courtyard to see if Netaji and Bhatkoo and Shamoo were doing fine. It seemed like Netaji's identity was still secret to the general public, and so we expected that all would be same at the courtyard of Netaji.

But when we arrived, the courtyard was covered with dirt and paper and plastic bags and other such rubbish that is on every street of Mumbai but never in the clean courtyard of Netaji. This could only mean that Netaji has not been doing his sweeping duties, and this made us worried.

Perhaps he ignored his sweeping due to many days of worry for us and for his servants, I told Iqbal.

But Netaji has endured many years of worry and stress and what-not, said Iqbal, and the worry does not affect him as is evidenced by his smooth skin that has no wrinkles.

That is true, I said.

Let us go inside and see what is the problem, said Iqbal.

We went to knock on the door, but when I knocked, the door pushed open and I could see that the lock had been broken. This created great worry for us, and we ran inside and shouted out for Netaji and Bhatkoo and Shamoo, but there was no answer whatsoever. Fearing the worst, we descended into the hydroponic underground, and when we arrived, we had to sit down due to shock.

All the hydroponics had been destroyed. The glass tanks and tubes and lights and tables were all broken and shattered, and the few plants that remained were dead. Suddenly I felt so sad for the plants, and now I understood why Netaji said they are alive and can understand us. I could feel they had suffered, and it made me angry at the people that must have done it.

Just then we heard a shout and a loud noise, and I turned just in time to move away from a stick that was addressed at my head. When I saw it was Bhatkoo doing the screaming and attempted hitting, I shouted at him and he immediately stopped.

Bhatkoo was in a sorry state. He was dirty and smelled of sweat and it looked like he had not eaten for one or two days. His eyes were big and red, and I felt he had not come out into the sunlight for those one or two days at least.

They took everything and everyone, he said with a mad look in his eyes.

Who, I asked.

Government, he said.

What government, I asked as I thought about the Israelis and Americans and Pakistanis.

Indian of course, said Iqbal.

Yes, said Bhatkoo. Netaji had made the double deal for the weapons with some government official, and because of the failure of the weapons deal, that government official has fallen out of favor with his party and was threatened and so he gave up the name and location of Netaji and said that Netaji had double-dealed with him and should be faulted.

So where is Netaji now, I asked.

I do not know, said Bhatkoo, because I have been hiding underground since the raid.

We must find him, I said.

Of course, said Iqbal, no question.

But how, said Bhatkoo, no one will know where he has been taken.

There is one person who will know, I said as I licked a remaining piece of salty spicy special bhaji from the outside of my mouth.

39

As predicted, the pao-bhaji-walla was able to help us. He did not personally know about the raid, but he had some contacts that he said would tell him anything under threat of being black-listed and not allowed to eat special bhaji from him.

By noon the next day we had the required information, and in addition the pao-bhaji-walla put us in touch with the brother of a contact of one of his contacts, and this third-degree contact would let us into this secret government holding area where they hold people based on the feelings of politicians and not on the principles of law.

The secret place was not far, but we had to take a bus there. I had taken Bhatkoo to my home and forced him to take bath and then my wife had fed him and given him clean kurta-pajama to wear, so he looked much better. And now that we would be going to at least talk to his master, he was in high spirits.

We will fight to the death to free him, said Bhatkoo.

There will be no fighting, I said.

No, said Iqbal, we are only here to talk.

Correct, I said, or else we will all get locked up and that will be the end of the matter.

Bhatkoo understood and kept quiet, and soon our bus stop arrived and we jumped from the bus. The secret place was actually a single-storey square building in the middle of a very busy marketplace, and I thought it was very artistic of the government to place it right there in between the sellers of spinach and eggplant and papaya. That way if the prisoner shouts for help, no one will hear because all the vegetable-sellers are shouting all the time in order to sell vegetables.

We gave the special agreed-upon coded knock on the door, and the door was opened quickly and we were brought in fast so that the door could be shut again. The inside of the place was very big and open, and there were no separate rooms or cells or anything like that.

Immediately we saw Netaji sitting on a bench at the back of the room, and behind him were Shamoo and some of the other attendants and members of Netaji's Hydroponic Institute for Foreign Policy.

Netaji was surprised and happy to see us, and we hugged each other and then sat down to talk. He looked to be in fine health, and not so worried at all, but then I remembered Iqbal's reminder that Netaji was not someone who got worried easily, and this is evidenced by his wrinkle-free skin.

Not to worry, he said to Bhatkoo and us, I will be free soon and things will be back to normal.

But the hydroponics are all destroyed, I said, and the courtyard is dirty.

Remember, he said, if there is no dirt then there is no need for the sweeper and certainly no need for the broom.

This was an inspirational statement worthy of a great wrinkle-free leader like Netaji Subhash Chandra Bose, and I stood up instinctively and saluted.

We are at your service Netaji, I said, and I no longer think you are a madman.

Or maybe now you are equally a madman, he said.

At this we all laughed, like how you laugh at something that may be true but should not be considered as a serious possibility.

But actually, said Netaji as he stood up and looked at me, it is more true to say that we will soon be at your service.

Means what, I said.

It is complicated, said Netaji, and you are just a simple bugger and so it will take time to explain.

Then better to start the explanation quickly, I said, because we only have fifteen more minutes before we will be thrown out of this place.

Now is not the time for such detailed explanations, said Netaji, but soon I will be home and we can talk in peace and privacy.

You will be freed from this place? said Bhatkoo in disbelief.

Even I was little bit doubtful. After all, it was a secret government facility, and since Netaji himself was a secret, this situation of captivity could go on indefinitely.

My friends, said Netaji, I have negotiated my way from

Taiwan to Japan to North Korea to China to Kashmir to Delhi to Kanpur to Calcutta and finally to Mumbai, which is now my home. My network of secret contacts stretches through all these places and even into some countries that you simple people have never heard of. You think I cannot negotiate my way out of this silly situation?

I had forgotten that our man Netaji was in fact a foreign relations and policy expert, and what is a foreign policy expert if not a masterful negotiator? In fact, the double and triple deals that took us on our Gandhian adventures should be enough proof, and I did not even know why I was worried.

Soon the politician whom I had arranged the arms deal with will be thrown out of his party, said Netaji, and his cousin will take his seat.

And you know his cousin, I said excitedly, and this cousin is your contact.

I know his cousin, said Netaji, but his cousin is actually quite a terrible bugger and I hate him and in fact he also hates me.

That does not sound good, I said, so how can that be to your benefit?

Netaji sighed and looked around.

Okay, he said, since you are forcing me to explain the whole situation I will do so.

Good, I said.

See, said Netaji, this cousin is actually such a terrible bugger that I have made contact with some other members of his party that hate this cousin. And in foreign policy they say that my enemy's enemy is my friend, and so I have automatically become friendly with these other members.

And they will release you, I said in delight.

Yes but not for free, said Netaji, because after all, a negotiation ends with some compromise and both sides must provide some item.

Of course, I said, and you will be providing what?

You, said Netaji, I will be providing you.

40

At first I assumed this was some agreement like that of master and servant for life or hopefully just for some short period of time. Perhaps I would have to do some cleaning or dusting or cooking or what-not for some politicians. Of course, none of these menial tasks were below my dignity. After all, Gandhiji himself once cleaned the dirty bathrooms of some politicians in order to make a point about something. And similarly I would clean things for these politicians in order to make my point and secure Netaji his freedom. But then a brainwave hit me and I knew there would have to be some limit.

But I cannot do any pornographic service, I said quietly.

At this Netaji laughed so loudly that the guard looked at us and made a sign for us to keep quiet or else he would throw out the visitors. I made a sign to the guard that we only needed a few more minutes and then we would be off, and he turned away from us and left us alone.

You are a silly funny bugger, he said, and this will come in handy during the campaign.

What campaign, I said.

RK-sahib, said Netaji, you will be put forth as a challenger in the upcoming elections. You will be contesting this terrible cousin for his seat, and I must see to it that you win. All my resources and skills will be put into use, and along with your brother in life Iqbal as an advisor, I have no doubt that the seat will be secured.

I do not think I fully understood what this Netaji was saying, and so I simply nodded and sat there in silence.

But I will have to go to office still, I said, and so all this must happen only in the evenings and on Sunday.

Netaji laughed again.

Forget your office now, he said, because you will be entering a new career.

What career is that? I said in confusion.

And at this point I felt a hand on my shoulder, and I looked up to see Iqbal, my brother in life, looking at me as if to say: Do not worry. I am there, no?

41

And so, my friends, this is the story of our Gandhian adventures. I cannot reveal many details about the campaign and what-not, because it is all classified information. Suffice it to say that my new career is very much in the Gandhian spirit, and my brother in life is now at my side in our new office in the government building in Mumbai.

Perhaps you people who are reading will now wonder and say that this does not seem like the end of the Gandhian adventures, and how can the Gandhian adventures end at this moment when surely it is like a beginning. And this is true in the sense that the pursuit is never complete, and the Gandhian, although passive, must never rest and wait for the truth to come. The Gandhian must go out and pursue the truth, wherever it may lie and whatever form it may take.

But this is also an ending because in some way we have completed one iteration of the eternally-repeating Gandhian cycle: first they ignore you, then they laugh at you, then they fight you, then they give up.

And then you win.

∞

a novel by
ZUBIN J. SHROFF
WWW.ZUBINJSHROFF.COM
3136 Hennepin Ave Apt #2
Minneapolis MN
55408-2626

CPSIA information can be obtained at www.ICGtesting.com
Printed in the USA
BVOW05s1314171014

371245BV00001B/5/P